Remember Me

Gabriel Fowler

BEACON
PUBLISHING GROUP

Remember Me

For information, or to order additional copies, please
contact:

Beacon Publishing Group
P.O. Box 41573 Charleston, S.C. 29423
800.817.8480| beaconpublishinggroup.com

Publisher's catalog available by request.

ISBN-13: 978-1-949472-63-9

ISBN-10: 1-949472-63-9

Published in 2019. New York, NY 10001.

First Edition. Printed in the USA.

Remember Me

Acknowledgements

To my parents, for always supporting me no matter what adventure I might decide to dive into. For that, I am truly thankful. Joel and Alicia, you're the best brother and sister the baby of the family could ever ask for, I love you. Grandma & Grandpa Fowler, it is because of your strength and love for one another that this story could be told. Thank you for reminding me what unconditional love really looks like. To the remaining family members, my hope is that this story, and the journey it may take you on, helps to not only guide you, but in some way brings you a moment of peace. Jeff and Val St. John and Heather Bergen, it has been a long road, but I certainly could not have done this without the love and support to keep writing that you three have shown me over the years.

Thank you to Micah Beltz, Kevin and Leah Stockwell, Greg Knight, Gonzo, Drew Gula, Duke and the whole Rye Berry crew; thank you for your friendship, laughter and support of this project. Thank you to Beacon Publishing Group and my editor Bobby Collins for taking a chance on this story and helping a decade long dream of mine finally come to fruition. And to writers like Khaled Hosseini, Brandon Sanderson and Dan Brown, for inspiring me to tell my story. A special thank you to Krista Gramens for using up the little free time you had to help illustrate and incredible book cover.

Sarah Fairbanks, your faith has blown me away since day one and you've inspired me to love others the way God has shared his love with the world. Your support of me, my passions, creativity and this project has been endless. I cannot thank you enough.

Remember Me

Chapter 1

"I couldn't tell you when I first realized she was forgetting. We all forget things, right? The pin to our credit card, even though we've been using it for the last six years. A grandbaby's birthday. A recipe for pie crust."

Allan was a man of eighty-six. Hunched in the shoulders, hips and knees made of plated metal, and glasses as thick as bulletproof windows. But humble, loving, and a God-fearing man. I had been a part of their story for three years. A news article about a woman found sitting on the stoop of an old, brick home in East Brooklyn caught my eye one morning as I sat in the office, thumbing through month old newspapers. Her hands and face were covered in dirt. She was wearing a white and purple bath robe, one slipper, and held a curling iron in her left hand.

Remember Me

Mary-Ann Cauldwell. Mama, as she was called in her neighborhood, spent most of her life caring for others. Whether it was at the soup kitchen she helped open with her best friend Sharice, or at the Big House, Mary-Ann didn't know any better than to wear a smile in the hopes of sharing it with someone else.

"There's only one of me," she'd say as she scooped a ladle full of gravy over mashed potatoes. "But God gave me a big enough heart to share it with those in need."

August 16, 2010. I sat in the second row of Helping Hands Baptist Church, the Big House, listening to Allan speak. Mary-Ann's casket, a chestnut oak with weaves of red running along the trim, sat before the stage. As a reporter, I often find myself so wrapped up in deadlines that I miss the emotion. Maybe I was better at it thirty years ago, but after thousands of stories, I end up rushing to get the work done because I know there is another story right around the corner. But, there was something about Allan, there was something about Mary-Ann, there was something about seeing how many people came to the Big House to say goodbye; that I turned off my recorder, stuffed my pen and pad back into my bag and just found myself being there.

"But when I found her that day on Ray McKinley's stoop, I knew something was wrong."

Allan dabbed his forehead with a white kerchief. His suit was bold. Violet with pinstripes from shoulder to heel. Underneath, he wore an orange vest over a black shirt and plum tie. On his feet were black, snakeskin loafers. 'I'm not a man of mourning anymore,' he told me one day. 'I'm a man of celebration.'

"I thank God she didn't stray too far," he said. A parade of 'amen' went about the room, followed by a hundred fan flaps, though those were likely more for the heat. "And that Ray was kind enough to wait with her until I arrived." The crowd looked left to where Ray was seated. He pinched his lips and gave a slight nod.

Allan wiped his head and neck before continuing. "I don't scare easy. And that's saying much 'cause I worked the iron yard for forty years, *and,* I've been a deacon here at this church for twenty-five. And we all know God's people got some problems." He smiled, looking over at Bishop Anderson.

"Yes, Lord," a woman shouted. Others laughed, and a wave of heat shot through the room.

"That day I realized what true fear was. I could say it grips you, tightening its chain around your neck making it hard to breath. But fear is a choice, and in that moment, I chose to feel helpless." Allan walked to the middle of the stage and sat on the top step. It was almost cliché. Cardboard cutout of the deceased face, a handful of bouquets placed on the stage and on top of the casket. A large sign where people could write loving notes sat on a stand nearby. But if you knew Mary-Ann and what she meant to this community… I felt that after three and a half years, she became Mama to me too.

Allan propped a leg up and rested his arm over his knee. "When I looked into my Mary-Ann's eyes that day I knew how wrong I was. God did not give us a spirit of fear, and he couldn't have proven that more clearly than he did through my wife." Several hands waved through the air accompanied by a shout of amen. "She wouldn't want to be remembered for much more than her smile, and her heart. I know she would only ask that each of you strive to bring joy to others in everything that you do." Allan stood slowly, walked down the steps and stood beside the casket. "It's funny how life works. Even in her most forgetful days, who she truly was as a person never really went away. I want to thank Sherry and Michael for coming." He stepped forward and took the hand of a petite, white woman in the front row.

"Their son Landon, because of his curiosity, became my wife's best friend during her last year here on this earth. He brought a piece of her spirit back, but more importantly, brought back her smile.

Their snow angels, card games and pirate adventures ended up being the last thing she remembered. I could not have asked for a better way for her to cross the finish line. And for that, I thank you." Landon stood and wrapped his arms around Allan's leg. Allan tenderly kissed his head, then pulled him away toward the casket. From his jacket, Landon removed a small snow globe and placed it on the stand, the tiny crystals falling weightless to the bottom.

Tears began to draw lines down Allan's cheeks. The fans stopped. The room fell silent save for the gentle whimper of a heartbroken husband. Landon found his way back to his seat as Bishop Anderson walked to Allan's side and placed an arm around his waist. Bishop gestured for the choir to begin singing as he walked Allan to the end of the pew. Allan cupped his hands over his face. His body jerked as the words of Mary-Ann's favorite hymn rang out.

Lord if I. Find favor in your sight. Lord please, hear my heart's cry. I'm desperately waiting, to be where you are. Across the hottest desert, I'll travel near or far.

The congregation stood, hands raised to the heavens as if helping to carry her spirit home. The chorus rang throughout the room with tears of worship and shouts of praise.

For Your glory. I will do anything. Just to see You. To behold You as my King.

As a fifty-three-year-old Italian Catholic, it's fair to say, that day I truly experienced God for the first time.

It's said that Alzheimer's is a disease that attacks the memory. Strips someone of remembering who they are and those around them. A disease that buries them inside their own mind. I like to think of Alzheimer's, not as someone losing their memory, but as those loved one's accessing memories they thought they had lost themselves. We sang until our eyes dried out and our voices strained for sound.

Her daughters, Carol and Stacey, stood at each end of the casket, while her sons, Aaron, Prince, Luke, and Paul, lifted their mother and carried her down the aisle. I took Allan by the arm and we followed close behind. The sun hung bright and a dusting of clouds speckled the pale blue sky. Six city blocks were barricaded as the hearse moved slowly toward Lucas Berry Cemetery, a tail of nearly a thousand people trailing behind.

"Mama's in heaven cooking up her famous cornbread and gravy," Bishop Anderson said as the casket was being lowered. "Jesus is gonna be in for a treat."

"Amen," someone from the crowd said. "Yes, Lord," said another.

Bishop Anderson took Allan's hand in his. "Second Corinthians tells us, 'Blessed be the God and Father of our Lord Jesus Christ, the Father of mercies and God of all comfort, who comforts us in all our affliction.' Let us pray."

Though I felt encapsulated by the moment, I pulled the thirty-five-millimeter camera Allan had given me as a Christmas gift in our second year and began taking shots. It felt like time had stopped. Or I was stuck in one of those movie voice-over scenes during the final credits where the camera slowly pans to a wide shot of a city scape, and someone is leaving you with a profound statement.

I made an entire album of that day as a gift to the family. Something they could always go back to when they found themselves forgetting. It's interesting how pain and loss bring people together and closer to a God they spend so much of their time trying to run away from.

By the time I made it back to Allan's house, the sun had fallen below the buildings. The evening train crunched overhead. The city had lulled to evening meals in front of the television. "It's good to see you again," Paul, the eldest, said as I entered the house. He was a gentle man with a kind smile underneath a handful of scars. 'An accident in the kitchen as a child,' was all I knew.

"It's good to see you too. Unfortunate it's under these circumstances." I hung my blazer over the back of a chair in the entryway.

"It was only a matter of time. She's in a better place sharing that smile with God's kingdom." Paul smiled again, his eyes telling of a sense of peace. "You've been here enough to know where things are. I'm sure the family that's still here would love to see you."

The hallway was scattered with family photos dating back to the early 1900s. My favorite was their wedding. Mary-Ann was nineteen, Allan twenty. Her face was thin. A sharp jawline that merge into a dimpled chin. 'It was the Native American in her,' Allan had said. Her eyes were wide with joy and her mouth sprung open in a smile that was truly a gift to this world. Allan looked almost embarrassed. When I asked him, he said it was because he just couldn't believe he'd gotten so lucky.

As I walked into the kitchen, I saw little pockets of people talking. Just behind the chatter was the sound of a record player playing Gladys Knight, *Neither One of Us Wants to be the First to Say Goodbye*. I walked to a small table with assorted cheese and fruit.

"Hey man, glad you made it," Aaron said, placing a firm hand on my shoulder. He was the busy bee of the family. Always working, but he sure took after his mother with that smile. "I gotta run. I'll catch up with you later." With an awkward wave, I watched as he disappeared down the hallway and out the front door.

The family room was where I had spent most of my time if I wasn't at the hospital observing Mary-Ann. A love seat wrapped in plastic sat to the right, a side table with a feathered lamp next to it and a coffee table in front. Two reclining chairs were straight ahead, angled just right to see the box television and bookshelf along the main wall. It was there I found Prince sitting in one of the chairs, cradling a cup in his arms. We had grown close during our time together, and though he didn't often show it, I could tell this whole thing was really hitting him hard.

"Hanging in there?" I asked, setting my plate down on the coffee table and finding a seat in the other chair. Prince shrugged and took a sip of gingered ale. "Your mother was an amazing woman Prince, she really was."

"She didn't remember any of us by the end," he said. A man in his fifties and nearly six feet five, Prince was certainly a gentle giant.

"I think her story isn't about what she remembered. I think it's more about what she helped others remember." It was hard to find any words, let alone the right ones in a situation like this; so, I sat back in the chair and allowed for silence. It was what he needed.

"When will your story be finished?" Prince asked after a long while.

"My deadline is in three months. But I should have the first draft done in the next couple of weeks."

"She would have liked to have read it." I saw his lips tightened into a thin line.

I fumbled forward in the chair and rested my arms on my legs. "I'm sure I'll find myself reading it to her by the grave."

"That'd be nice," he said.

"There he is," a voice said from the other room. Allan burst through a handful of people with a napkin in his hand and a weathered smile across his face. "I wasn't sure if you were going to make it back."

"I wouldn't have been able to live with myself if I hadn't. The photographs can wait, and the story isn't done without an ending." I got up from my seat and greeted him with a hug. "I swear you're the only man in this world that could pull that suit off." Allan let out an airy laugh, coughing several times into his elbow.

"You're too much Sal. Mary-Ann sure would have liked you in her early days. I'm sure glad I got to her first." He laughed again, this time grabbing me around the neck and pulling me in tight, laying a friendly kiss on the top of my head.

"I'd like to bring over the photographs sometime next week. Let you pick the ones you'd like to see in the book," I said, pulling away.

"I would like that," he said. "But speaking of endings. I had an idea."

"What's that?"

"I'm not sure what yet. But, that boy Landon, I'd like to do something special for him in her name." Allan rubbed his chin in thought.

"I think that sounds like a wonderful idea. Take some time to think about it and when I swing by next week, we can talk more." He held out his hand and I shook it firmly.

"You're off huh?" he asked.

"I think that'd be best. I'd like to get home before it gets too late." I hugged him again, his bristled chin rubbing coarsely against my cheek.

"Take care. Thank you for everything," Allan said as I pulled my coat over my shoulders and trudged back outside. The moon lit the ground in spots as I walked to the R train. The forty-minute ride gave me time to jot down some thoughts on the day and how I wanted to steer the story to a close.

A beautiful woman with long, brown hair, freckles and a red trench coat sat across from me. Her eyes were glued to her phone, smiling at a video and bobbing her head slightly from left to right. It's amazing how much of the world they miss out on, and it only seems to be getting worse.

I arrived back at my one-bedroom condo to the wagging tail and wet tongue of my pit mix, Scout. Cracking open a beer, I sat by the window watching the city fall asleep and wake up all at the same time. I wasn't much of a sleeper. My doctor told me it would eventually catch up to me, but I figured if I didn't work myself to death; a bus, cab, or train would.

I walked into my studio, a twelve-by-twelve spare bedroom I converted into an art room with a pop-up dark box. A sketch table sat in the right corner, a desk with a typewriter was positioned next to a small closet filled with art supplies. Sliding doors led to a small balcony where on a cloudless night, the sky lit up like New York City itself. After hanging a few photos, I sat down to start the last chapter.

Chapter 2

November 2007

Snow gently layered the sidewalk as I walked into Benny's Diner. Allan agreed to meet me for breakfast to talk about the story I was hoping to write. I asked for a coffee and bowl of oatmeal. Allan ordered two pancakes, bacon and an orange juice.

We talked for hours, or rather he did, his voice slow and melodic. His words were poignant, and I clung to them like a rock climber grips a handhold. As I watched him through the steam that rose from my coffee mug, I felt as though I were standing there with him, on the streets of Brooklyn in the summer of 1944.

"Dust clouds danced in the air as garbage trucks and cars drove down the busy streets. I stared up at the unfinished buildings, the sound of sledgehammers pounding away. It wouldn't be long before I was up there on those beams myself."

Allan looked out the window and smiled. "This diner's been here for over seventy years. I'd stop in every day for lunch. Nickel sandwiches and penny sodas."

"That was your first job?" I asked, scooping a spoonful of oatmeal into my mouth.

"Well, I'd done newspaper routes, and cut grass as a boy. But, this was the first job I had that really meant something." He tugged lightly on the left strap of his overalls. "Once I realized the work would never stop, I decided to stay. Retired just before I turned sixty."

"That's arduous work to be doing for forty years," I said. The bell on the door rang and a man and woman walked in.

Allan chuckled, sucking on his teeth. "I've never looked at it that way. If you do a job well and you love it, it's not hard work at all."

I thought for a moment about my own job. The years I'd spent arguing and stressing over what font to use, or which story was more important for front page. How ironic, that a man hunched, hips replaced, and walking with a cane had an *easier* job than I did at times.

"Don't get me wrong, there are parts of the job I could have done without. But I'm grateful for what I learned," Allan said.

"How is everything Mr. Cauldwell? Mr.—"

"Pitello," I said to the waitress.

14

"Everything is mighty good Jackie. How's the new house?" Allan asked, turning in his seat.

"I love it," she said excitedly. "My husband keeps finding things to complain about, but I think that's because he doesn't know how to fix them. Kids love it too. Eloise said just the other day that it's like living in a castle. Ha. It's only a three bedroom, but I guess compared to the apartment." Jackie began to fidget with the pad and pen in her apron pocket.

"That's lovely Jackie," Allan said.

"How's Mary-Ann doing? We all miss her around here," she asked, pulling the pen out and twirling it between her fingers.

"Okay I guess. Doctor says it affects each person differently."

"I was so sad when I heard she was starting to forget things. But I'll never forget that smile. It was your Mary-Ann that helped me get this job and get me and the kids out of that shelter. My husband was running all over the city trying to get hired. It's so hard for someone with a criminal record to find people that will take a chance on them, and he's been clean for years. I always say it was all that praying your Mary-Ann was doing that helped him get the janitor job at the law firm. Now he's managing his own crew." Jackie seemed out of breath and her face blushed a soft rose. "Oh, there I go again. Talking up all your time."

"Don't be bothered," Allan said with a wink.

I'm not sure if I'd ever seen someone that was so good at listening. Must be why his marriage lasted so long.

"God is good," Allan said.

"All the time," Jackie said in return. "Enjoy the rest of your meal. Give Mary-Ann my love." With that, Jackie walked to the next table.

"Now that's the Mary-Ann I'd like to know," I said, pulling my pen and pad from my bag.

Allan nodded his head slowly, allowing for a moment of silence. "I was walking home from my first day in the iron yard. My hands were covered in grease and I had black streaks running down the sides of my blue overalls. Doc Eckers had said if I worked hard as a cleaner, he'd give me a shot in the assembly. I lived near eighty-fifth and a hundred and fourth, just a block from Forest Park. I didn't know it at the time, but Mary-Ann's mother worked in the salon on a hundred and third. I stopped here at the diner for a glass of water and a piece of pie before heading home for the night. And there she was, standing outside the salon with two of her friends. Her hair curled and bounced just above her shoulders. She was wearing a red blouse, a blue skirt and white gloves that went almost to her elbows, you know, like the ones girls wear to

16

church. Her lips matched her shirt and I could see her bright smile from across the street as she laughed." Allan paused. His eyes were closed, and he was smiling, the image dancing vividly in his mind. I set my pen down and quickly took a picture with my phone.

"I don't believe I would have made much of an impression had I not been hit by the car as I wandered aimlessly into the street." He stopped to laugh.

"You were hit by a car?" I asked, quickly making a note.

"I sure was. Stepped right out in front of it, eyes glued to that girls pretty smile and smack," he said, clapping his hands together. "When I came too, she was crouching over me, fanning my face. She asked if I was alright and I told her it would take all the pain away if she let me take her to a movie. I'd believed for a long time that she only said yes because she'd felt bad for me. But, after so many years of marriage and six children, I'd say she fell in love. Don't know why, the clumsy fool I am. But hey, I'll forever be grateful she did."

Allan slid his plate to the end of the table. The diner had a steady stream of people in and out. Some sat for meals, others jawed with the owner at the front as they drank their morning coffee before work. It was everything I thought a diner should be.

"How long was it before you got married?" I asked. My coffee had gotten cold, so I set it to the side.

"About five months is all. I knew I had to scoop her up before she changed her mind. My mama was real happy the first time I brought her around the house. Told me she was an angel sent from heaven and if I screwed things up, God would strike me dead where I stood." Allan itched the back of his neck and smiled.

"Well you aren't dead yet," I said playfully.

"You all finished?" Jackie said as she walked back to the table.

"Yes ma'am," Allan said.

"You should stop with all that ma'am nonsense. Makes me feel old." Jackie giggled, a curl of her brown hair falling out from under her hairnet and over her left temple. She took our plates back to the kitchen and returned with the bill. "Mitch said enjoy your day. It was nice meeting you, Mr. Pitello," she said as she left.

I was about to pull my wallet from my pants when I noticed the bill was just a piece of paper that said, 'We love you Al, and we are praying for you and your family.' I sat back in the booth and exhaled. Part of me wanted to jump up and down. I had found a jackpot story and I was only a few hours into my investigation. But there was something else tugging at me. Something real.

Something that told me, this will be more than just a story. I thanked Allan for taking the time to meet me and he agreed to meet again at the end of the week.

"Come by the house and I'll introduce you to my wife and one of my sons, Aaron. He has his own business selling antiques, but he's been helping me take care of Mary-Ann as of late," he said with a handshake.

"I can't wait," I said with a wave.

New York City is filled with stories. Walk a half-block and you'll have passed a dozen. Some as simple as, 'this is the place where so-and-so found a five-dollar bill.' Others as heartbreaking as, 'this is where so-and-so got shot.' And some as profound as, 'this is where Malcolm X stood when he was recruiting for the Black Panther Movement.'

I walked the city for an hour, trying to imagine what some of those stories were, while also watching other stories develop. People climbing on and off buses, buying food from kiosks and listening to music, ignoring their surroundings.

◇

Allan greeted me with a hug when I got to the porch outside their small, two-bedroom, brick home. I walked into the house to the smell of apple pie and Aaron waving a small, white towel through the air, hoping to avoid the fire alarm from going off. He threw the towel over his shoulder and met me halfway down the hallway.

"How are you doing? I'm Aaron," he said, thrusting his hand into mine.

"Sal Pitello. I'm well, thank you," I said.

"My pops told me a little about what you'd like to do. You know, my mother means a lot to me and a lot to this community. So, don't go around shaming her in any way." He threw a friendly smile in at the end, but I knew he wasn't joking.

"You have my word," I said quickly, my palms beginning to sweat. Aaron talked through a few of the photographs on the wall and led me into the living room before returning to the kitchen.

Mary-Ann sat in the love seat wrapped in a blanket with her hands on her lap. She was watching *Let's Make a Deal* and mumbling, 'mm, he's so fine,' whenever Wayne Brady was on the screen. "I keep telling myself that she thinks that's me." Allan laughed and motioned for me to sit. It wasn't until I did that Mary-Ann noticed I was there.

"Hello darlin, are you here to fix the roof?" she said. Her voice was soft and pleasant. "No, Mary-Ann," Allan said, grabbing hold of her hand. "This is the man I was telling you about. The one who is going to write a story about you. Do you remember?" Allan leaned in and kissed her cheek.

"Oh yes. Right. The one from the newspaper. Mr. Pitello. You didn't tell me he was bald. Not that it makes much of a difference, but it would have been nice to know." Allan looked at me and shrugged. "Is that apple pie I smell? I better go in the kitchen and make sure it doesn't burn." Mary-Ann threw the blanket off, climbed to her feet and walked into the kitchen.

"She's always been good with names, but I only said yours once, and that was three days ago." Allan smiled widely. "It's moments like that, that get me excited."

From the other room, we heard a plate crash against the floor. "Don't worry about it, Mom. Just go back into the living room and sit with dad and the man from the newspaper." Aaron held her arm as he led her back to the love seat.

"His name's Mr. Pitello," she said sharply as Aaron walked away. Aaron threw his hands in the air and laughed.

"I'd like to start by saying thank you for allowing me to come here today," I said, extending a hand to hold hers. "Amy, my chief of staff, agreed to a three-page spread in our May release, but I spoke with K&A Publishing and they agreed to fund a project for a minimum of sixty-five thousand words."

Mary-Ann's eyes opened wider. "And you're going to write all that, about me?" She pulled her hand slowly away and gazed off to the side. "I never thought my life would be interesting enough to write about."

"Think of it as your journey through life. The connections you've made, the impact you've had on others and what other families who are dealing with the same—" Allan's grip on my arm was like a vice. The pain shot through my forearm in both directions. My head snapped to him as I tried to wrench free. His eyes were wide and he pulled me into the other room. If I hadn't known how old he was, I would have thought he was in his thirties and part of some professional athletic team the way he dragged me to the kitchen.

"What the hell is going on?" I said, rubbing my arm.

"She doesn't know," Allan said through clinched teeth.

"Why did you all leave?" Mary-Ann shouted.

"Don't worry sweetheart. We'll be right back," Allan said.

"What do you mean she doesn't know? She was found on the stoop of a friend's house four blocks away. You've taken her to doctors. She has to know something." I looked down at my arm and could see the marks his fingers made.

"The doctor said that the easy part would be telling her about the condition. But the hard part would be convincing her that it's true. So, we left it alone and are dealing with it in our own way." Allan leaned against the wall, his head glistening with sweat.

Aaron shook his head. "I tried to convince him that we should at least try, but he wasn't hearing any of it."

I took several deep breaths and said, "I understand that it's a family decision, but don't you think it would have been a good idea to let *me* know before I ruined it, nearly losing an arm in the process."

"Mr. Pitello. I'm sorry. You're right, I should have told you the other day at the diner." Allan walked to the fridge and poured two glasses of ice water, handing one to me.

"Thank you. Now that that's settled, I'd like to go back in there and ask her a few questions." Allan nodded and we returned to the living room. Mary-Ann's focus was back on the television.

"I'm going to turn this off now. Mr. Pitello would like to ask you a few questions," Allan said, clicking the remote.

"Mr. who?" Mary-Ann asked, tucking the blanket under her legs.

"Mr. Pitello. The man from the newspaper," Allan said. Mary-Ann nodded her head as if she remembered.

I took a small recorder from my bag and placed it on the coffee table. "November twenty-fourth. Nine fifty-three a.m. Tell me, Mrs. Cauldwell. How many children do you have and what are their names?"

Mary-Ann thought for a moment, her lips curling into a tender smile, as if remembering what it felt like to hold each one for the first time. "Well, there's Paul," she started. "He's my eldest son. Such a nice boy. Kind to everyone." She paused, her brow coming together at the bridge of her nose. "I should have been paying closer attention that day. I should have—" She cut off, her eyes beginning to well. Allan stood and wiped her cheeks with his thumbs, whispering in her ear.

"Luke, he was next," she continued. "Bossy too. He always had his brothers and sisters in line. Made it easier on me and Allan. Then there was Carol. She loved to be in everyone's business. Her favorite thing to say was, 'um, you won't believe what such-and-such did." Mary-Ann laughed, slapping her thigh. "Stacey was the fun one. Could spin your frown upside down. She didn't care much for nothing but a laugh and a shout. Now Aaron, he's the 'I'll sleep when I'm dead type.' I swear if he was paid for every minute he was actually working, he'd be a millionaire. He got my smile though, and people just fell in love." Aaron stuck his head around the corner and shared a bright, white smile.

"They say the last one always gets forgotten. But not me. Not my Prince. He'd strut around the house like he owned the place and I'd be lying if I said it wasn't true. He just kept growing too... Prince didn't have it easy though. Being the youngest of six can be hard, especially when your brothers are that much older than you. But boy could he sing." Mary-Ann sank down in her seat.

The strain of remembering stretched across her face. I leaned forward and stopped the recorder. "This is going to really help me get started," I said. "I will call you soon to set up another time to meet."

"You're not going to stay for a piece of pie?" Aaron said in the doorway.

"I really wish I could, but I have three stories to revise and a meeting at eleven." I stood and made my way to Mary-Ann's side. Kneeling, I squeezed her shoulder gently and thanked her for her time.

"Take one for the road then," Aaron insisted, placing a slice into a ziplocked bag.

"Thank you. And thank you again, Allan. This is a great start. I'll be in touch."

Chapter 3

January 2008

I had just read an email from my brother Mike and hopped in the shower when my phone rang. Assuming it was work, I let it go to my voicemail. As I climbed off the elevator and out into the frigid winter air, I froze, much like the icicles that hang from the sides of buildings. Pressing the keypad on my phone, I huddled by the door and listened to the message again.

Hi. Mr. Pitello. This is Prince. Prince Cauldwell. We sat down several weeks ago to talk about my mother. Well, I just wanted to let you know that we are at Faith Memorial Hospital.

Mama's had a minor stroke. I thought maybe, if you wanted to come by and see her. F-for your story. I don't know. I just thought you should know.

Prince was as big and gentle as everyone had said. He and his wife owned their own business providing tech support for vet hospitals across the country, and he took some time away to see his mother and speak with me about my project.

"I don't want to say that I was her favorite," he had said, pulling the onions off his burger. "But she and I clung to each other for a long time. I still remember her staying up with me when I was seventeen and cramming for finals. I had a bad head cold and she'd run back and forth to the bathroom to make sure the cloth she held on my neck stayed cool. Not to mention I had three performances that weekend and a few directors from the college were going to be in attendance. Yeah, she was my rock."

I rushed through the ankle-deep snow to the bus stop, hopped onto the 22 and headed west toward the hospital. Hospitals were and still aren't a place I would normally go running too. After making the hard decision eight years ago to let my father go, I avoided them as much as I could.

As I walked through the main entrance, everything came back to me. The sound of muffled voices in the waiting room. The smell of sterilized equipment. The look on a young nurse's face as she ran down the hallway, her hands gripping the ends of her stethoscope. Even the orange glow of the exit signs above the doors sent ripples across my skin.

It's for the story, I told myself, stopping at a desk to ask where I could find the Cauldwell family.

Prince sat next to his brother Aaron outside the room. He was slouched in his seat with a leg propped up on his knee, while Aaron typed away on his phone, ignoring the passing hospital beds and sick patients.

"How is she doing?" I asked as I approached.

Prince sat up quickly, wiping his face with his hands. "She's alright. Pops said she slid out of her seat like a wet noodle. Her eyes rolled back and she lost consciousness." He paused to look at his brother. "Aaron carried her to the car and dad called ahead to let them know they were coming."

Aaron flipped his phone shut and looked up. He seemed as old as his father just then. White bristles covered his cheeks and chin in a thin beard and his eyes sunk deep in his head. He looked a man lost at sea; but he still smiled, this time with more effort.

"The doctor said he'd like to keep her here for a few nights, but she should make a 'full' recovery," Aaron said. "She'll need help regaining the strength in her legs."

The door to her room swung open and a petite, blonde nurse with a dimpled chin and horizon grey eyes stepped out. Her face was flush, her hands balled into tiny fists and she took several slow, calming breaths. "I can't do my job if he is going to be in there acting like that. Can one of you please explain to him that I need two vials of blood, so we can run more tests?" She turned and went back into the room. Aaron followed behind. I sat with Prince listening to Allan jaw back and forth with his son.

"He's taking it pretty hard," I said.

"You're telling me. I don't blame him. He's spent the last sixty years with her and now he has to watch her slowly disappear. I can't say I would react much differently." Prince shook his head slowly.

"Don't you remember what we talked about?" I asked, unwrapping a piece of gum. "This time with her will mean less if you focus on how she's changing, and not on the amazing life she lived. You'd be saying the last seventy years meant nothing."

"I hear you, but if it doesn't make it any easier for me, it definitely won't make it any easier for him." Prince stood and stretched his arms over his head. "Would you like to go in and see her?" he asked.

The shades were pulled closed. The small lamp next to her bed was only a dim glow, shadows spreading like branches across the room. The walls were blue. The floor, a cold white tile. The nurse was just finishing the second vial when Allan turned and saw me. I tried to share a comforting smile but the tears that streamed down his face were like bullets, each one finding their way to his heart.

Mary-Ann looked peaceful beneath the tubes. Her eyes were closed, and her chest rose and fell as the air passed gently through her nose. It may have just been me, but it looked as though her lips were curled ever so gently at the corners.

We all sat in silence for a long time, only the sound of her heart monitor beeping in the background. My phone buzzed. Looking down, I saw that it was a text from Ryan, one of the copy editors, updating me on a story.

"You don't have to stay here all day," Prince whispered. I looked up from my phone and nodded.

"It's likely she'll be asleep till tomorrow morning. They gave her a sedative to help her rest. I just didn't know, with the story and all."

"No, of course. I'm glad you called. There's always something that can be used. If her condition changes, or you take her home, be sure to let me know." I leaned over and whispered in Prince's ear. "Make sure your father gets something to eat, okay?" Prince shook his head and Aaron walked me out into the hallway.

"What did you mean by 'there's always something that can be used?'" he said, leaning against the door.

"Aaron. I know you're not fully on board yet with this whole thing, but I promise, I won't write anything that will affect you or your family in a negative way. People love a story about families coming together," I said, placing a hand on his shoulder. "And the fact that you are here with Allan, sitting bedside to your sick mother goes a long way to not only sell books, but relay to this community how much you all care."

"That's fair," he said, nodding his head and walking back into the room.

I pulled my coat tight around my neck as I walked out. Sheets of snow fell from the sky so thick I could hardly see my hand in front of my face. I followed a shallow set of footprints down the sidewalk and back to the bus stop.

"What took you so long?" Ryan said, walking into my office behind me. "I was at the hospital."

"Shit. Is everything alright?" he asked, taking a seat.

"It wasn't me. It was Mary-Ann Cauldwell. She had a minor stroke and her son called to let me know." Ryan looked at me sideways. "The story I'm writing about Alzheimer's for the May send-out."

"Oh right. The deal you made with K&A."

I hung my coat over my chair and sat down. "Yeah, that one. What is this?" I asked, lifting a small, thin box.

Ryan smiled, the way he always did when he was up to something. "It's a laptop computer," he said, holding his hands up to stop me from talking. "Look, I know we can't convince you to get one for your house, but you've gotta use one here in the office. It's 2008 man, the world is changing, and you have to understand that it's a hassle having to wait for you to get us your work. With this, you can just attach your story to an email and in seconds, I'll have it." He threw his arms in the air as if he had just invented the cure for cancer.

"Do you know how long it's going to take me to learn all of this."

"That's where you're wrong. If you only use it for writing your stories and sending them to Kendal and me, I can teach you in ten minutes."

This is what we get for hiring a twenty-something straight out of college. "Fine. But I swear if I have to call you every five minutes because I can't figure out what the hell I'm doing, you're going to watch me light this thing on fire."

"Deal," Ryan said, slapping his hand on the desk.

I reluctantly opened the box, not having any feelings of Christmas morning. I had seen them around for years, but the thought of having to learn about its usage was daunting. But to my surprise, it only took him eight minutes and forty-three seconds, (yes, I timed him), to explain the basics of Microsoft Word and how to attach a file to my email.

"You shouldn't, but let me know if you run into trouble," he said as he left.

I spent the next fifteen minutes fiddling around with some of the other options before I realized I may actually enjoy the damn thing.

◇

"Hello, may I speak with Ms. Sharice?"

"This is her, who's calling?"

"My name is Sal Pitello. I'm a writer down at the Star Tribune. I was hoping I could speak with you about Mary-Ann Cauldwell." I spun a pen across my knuckles, then tapped it on the notepad on my desk.

"You're the man who's been leaving messages on my answering machine."

"Yes. I'm sorry. It's just that you two opened the soup kitchen together and I thought who better to get an idea of who Mary-Ann was than her best friend."

"Well, I don't get over there very often anymore. My daughter Alise runs the place but I know they miss seeing Mary-Ann."

I made a quick note about her daughter, circling her name several times. "Would it be too much to ask if I could meet you there to talk?"

"I suppose that would be alright," she said through a sigh. "I'll try to be there on Friday before lunch. That way I can welcome the people in as they arrive."

I looked over my calendar. I'd have to cancel my dentist appointment and send someone else to the ribbon cutting ceremony at the park. "That sounds great. I will swing by on Friday."

"Before lunch," she said.

"Yes, before lunch."

"Good. I'll expect you to help me at the front door," she said with a laugh. "I think that's a fair trade. Take care and I'll see you Friday."

◇

The face of the brick building was covered in artwork. A forest landscape stood in the background with a river running along the trees. Famous black figures in history held hands and carried signs that read, *Freedom* and *Equality,* along a dirt path. Martin Luther King Jr. led the march, with Harriet Tubman on his left and James Baldwin to his right. Above the door was a large sign painted red and black that said, *Full Bellies Soup Kitchen.*

As I entered, a young woman walked up and handed me a shovel. "Ms. Sharice said get to work," she said with a smile. I chuckled, slipping my gloves back on. I piled the snow in an alley to the left of the building and went back inside, tapping my boots on the door. I could hear the clang of pots and the soft thump of music coming from the kitchen. Setting the shovel against the wall, I made my way to the swinging door. A half-dozen women in hair nets swayed back and forth, waving ladles and spatulas through the air as they sang.

Gabriel Fowler

"So, you've met my daughter?" a voice said behind me.

I turned to find the woman who had handed me the shovel pushing Sharice in a wheelchair. She smiled widely.

"I certainly did," I said, wiping my forehead with the back of my hand. "And she put me right to work."

"As she should have," Sharice said. Her fingers were frozen in fists and she'd lost sight in her left eye, but beneath the wrinkles and drooping features, I could see that she had once been a stunning woman. "Go on and wash your hands. I know the girls would love some help in the kitchen before the place fills up." Alise wheeled her mother back across the cafeteria and into a room.

"You better hurry up and start washing those potatoes," Katrina, one of the women said. She was in her mid-forties, had wide hips, a cleft lip and a tattoo of a pair of angel wings on the back of her neck.

"Yes ma'am," I said with a laugh, rolling up my sleeves and plunging them into the cold water. "So how long have you been helping here?" I asked, scrubbing the potatoes and handed them off to be cut and dropped into a pot of boiling water.

"I've been coming here since I was eight years old. My momma was in and out of prison and I've never met my father. Sometimes in the summer

37

I'd have lunch and dinner here. Started volunteering as a sophomore in high school and I haven't left since." Katrina was like a machine with the knife, quartering each potato before I could get her the next one.

"So, Mary-Ann and Ms. Sharice were a big part of your life?"

"Oh yes. Mama, she let me and my sister stay with them for a few months so we didn't have to sleep in the car. They fed us, bought us clothes and gave us lunch money for school. I don't know what would have happened to us if they hadn't been there." Katrina wiped her head with her forearm and set the knife down to clean off the counter top.

I finished the potatoes and moved to a large square island to help make peanut butter and jelly, and ham sandwiches. "What about some of the other ladies?" I asked, turning back over my shoulder.

"Most of us have a very similar story. Abusive homes, poor neighborhoods, parents in and out of the house. Maxine," she said, pointing to a short woman with beautiful, light brown skin, and a scar that ran from her elbow to the palm of her hand. "Her father kicked her out the house when she was fourteen. Said if she wasn't going to bring home some money, she couldn't stay. She wound up on Sharice's doorstep with a shattered arm and two bullet holes in her shoulder." I looked over at

Maxine who was stirring a large pot of gravy, her hips snapping back and forth to the sound of Michael Jackson. If I hadn't been told; if she didn't bear the scars, I would never have guessed the life she endured.

"What happened?"

Katrina dried off her hands and moved to the island to work alongside me. "Pimp got ahold of her and when she refused, he broke her arm. She tried to run, but he gunned her down. One of the strongest women I've ever met. She crawled eight blocks in the middle of the night to Sharice's front porch." She shook her head and I could see she was trying to hold back tears. I realized I was doing the same.

I think that was the start. The start of me realizing how much of the world I was missing out on. I had done a feature story about a kid who was gunned down. I flew out to California to write about the riots in the 80s. I'd even sat in the courtroom when the Juice was on trial for double homicide. I'd done it all. But, nothing up to that point felt all that real to me.

"What brings you in here?" Katrina asked. "It's not every day a bald, white man shows up to lend a hand." She let out a heavy, chest rattling laugh. A few of the other women turned to look and I could feel the blood rise in my cheeks. "Don't mind them, they're all jealous I get to work with you," she said a little louder. The women sighed sarcastically and turned away.

"I'm a journalist for the Star Tribune. I'm writing a story on Mary-Ann's life and the struggles her family are having now that she's been diagnosed with Alzheimer's."

"Hmm. So sad. Mama was the light of this place for so long. Shame she won't remember all she's done."

"But you will," I said, flipping the last slice of bread over.

"Yes, that's right. I imagine she'll find a spot up on the wall too," she said.

The kitchen began to empty as the women brought the food out into the cafeteria. Ms. Sharice and I met at the front and she asked me to hold the door open.

"Be sure you say our famous words when they walk through," she said, raising a fragile hand in the air. "Hope You're Ready to Fill that Belly." Her mouth opened into an infectious smile.

"Hope you're ready to fill that belly," I said softly as the first person approached. The look on their face was one of confusion. Mine, I assume looked just as out of place.

"You gotta say it so it means something," Sharice said.

It took some time, but I eventually loosened up. I shook hands with some, hugged others and soon said the words as if I had been doing it all my life. We closed the doors at noon to a packed cafeteria bustling with laughter. I made my way around the room, introducing myself and learning a bit more about the people of East Brooklyn, and the impact *Full Bellies* has had on the community.

I met a veteran who had been homeless for over twelve years. A mother and daughter that lived in the shelter run by the church. Looking at the little girl, I pictured Katrina at the same age. Tattered clothes, knotted hair and head plunged into her mother's side, weary of strangers. By the end of lunch, I felt the muscles in my back and thighs tighten. It was more physical work than I'd done in years.

"You did well," Sharice said as I sat.

"Thank you. I'm glad I came." Sweat dripped off my arms and onto the floor. Alise pushed her mother up to the table, locked the wheels and walked to the kitchen to help clean.

"September 1937," Sharice started. "We were in fifth grade at Jefferson Elementary. I still remember her pigtail braids and red lunch pail as she sat down the first day. I was new to the school and she was the first one to say hello. Mouth wide as a river and teeth white as snow."

Katrina brought over two cups of water and a small plate of food. I nibbled, listening as intently as I had the first time I sat down with Allan.

"We were attached at the hip. My mother said there wasn't a day that went by that we weren't at one house or the other. We were the dainty type, dressing dolls up in our homemade fabrics, and braiding each other's hair. We even wore the same outfits to school. Our teachers would say one name and we'd both turn around. We were twins born from different wombs. Help me, would you?" she asked, gesturing at the water. I lifted the cup to her lips and wiped her face with a napkin when she finished. "That was until she met Allan?" I asked, putting her cup back on the table.

"You'd be dead wrong," she said with a laugh. Her hair bounced in curls around her brow. "For a while there, I'd go on dates with them. Got Allan all bent out of shape when Mary-Ann would pay more attention to me than she would him. He was good for her though. Kind, sweet. Dumb as a bucket of stones, but he'd have done anything for her. I made a deal with him one day." Sharice coughed.

"A deal?"

"Yes. I told him that he could have her as long as he didn't move away. We'd talked about opening a place together, to help our folk get back on their feet, times being what they were."

"You interested in a piece of pie, Mr. Pitello?" Katrina asked from the kitchen.

"No, thank you," I said, turning back to Sharice.

Her eyebrows narrowed, and she snickered. "You're gonna have to learn how things work around here if you plan on coming back. When someone asks you if you want dessert, it's not a question, it's more of a warning that it's coming." She smiled and shook her head in sympathy.

"Here you are," Katrina said, sliding a plate in front of me. "Key lime. Hope you like it."

"See. I told you," Sharice said. It was sour, but made my mouth salivate and it was gone before Sharice could continue talking.

"When did you open this place?" I asked, wiping my face.

Sharice thought for a moment before saying, "Full Bellies doors opened in 1953, but we got started in my parent's garage in '46. Boiled hot dogs for lunch. Mac and Cheese and ground beef for dinner. We gave out over four thousand meals in our first year."

"Wow. That's incredible. How were you able to fund the project?"

"The church helped us out for a while. Then we considered how we could turn it into a non-profit, you know, like some of those shelters. They gave us the run-around, saying, 'black folk should get jobs and not rely on the government so much. Funny thing is, half of the people that walked through our doors were white." Sharice took a deep breath, as if still releasing the stresses of early America for blacks.

"I'm sure I can use common sense to understand the meaning behind the name Full Bellies, but is there any other significance?" I asked, taking a sip of water.

"Mary-Ann can tell you the story, but really we just wanted to make sure people left with their bellies full. But more importantly, Mary-Ann wanted their hearts full." Sharice held her hands over her heart, her eyes bubbling with tears.

"You two have done an excellent job over the years," I said, placing a hand on her arm. "I'll make sure whoever reads the story knows that."

"Make sure you get in there that Mary-Ann was a snob and loved to boss people around too," she snickered.

"I sense there was a little tension between you."

"Only the kind best friends of over fifty years would have." Her smile faded slightly. "I hope she's not upset I haven't been by to see her. I'm not sure how I would react if she didn't recognize me is all."

I sat in silence for a moment. "I should head into the office for the afternoon." I stood, again feeling the soreness in my legs. "You shouldn't wait too long though. There *will* come a day when she doesn't."

Sharice nodded, then yelled for Alise to come bring her home. "I hope you'll come back here again."

"Of course. I'm sure there's a photo album or two you could take me through," I said, leaning down to give her a hug.

"Have a blessed day, Mr. Pitello," Katrina said, standing in the doorway of the kitchen drying her hands with a towel. "Hope to see you soon."

"Hope to see you soon!" a few of the other women shouted mockingly from the kitchen. Katrina turned to throw the towel and the room rumbled with laughter.

The cool afternoon air hit my lungs as I stepped outside. Cars drove by sloshing wet snow up onto the sidewalk. Pigeons squawked as I walked, and I looked back at the mural, imagining both Mary-Ann and Sharice walking side-by-side.

Chapter 4

Spring 2008

I sat in my car listening to 80s rock, looking out at Allan and Mary-Ann as they sat on their front porch. The early stages of spring were beginning to show itself and a few small clusters of snow were scattered across the ground. Paint chipped away from the posts and the gutter was filled with half thawed leaves.

Mary-Ann rocked back and forth in her chair smiling. She wore a light grey sweater and wrapped her legs in a blanket. Her eyes wandered as if seeing things for the first time. Allan was hunched forward in a black button up, grey slacks and a pair of slippers on his feet. He sipped on hot tea as he spoke. I could tell he was repeating himself by the way Mary-Ann would drift, only to return to him with a quick, snap of her head. I rolled down the windows and turned the radio off, catching the last half of the conversation.

"...wasn't my idea in the first place," Allan said, setting his cup on the railing. "Brandon was sure they would give us a seat. You tried to warn him." Allan giggled. He reached over and placed his hand on Mary-Ann's lap. "Right?"

"Hmm," she mumbled, looking over at him. "You're not Brandon. You're my Allan," she said, squeezing his hand.

"Yeah, that's me. But Brandon almost got us killed, remember?"

"Oh, yes. Down at Bailey's Burgers on eighty-third. We tried to warn him. They didn't want no niggers in there. Not unless they were sweeping the floor or washing the dishes. And even then, we were to keep to ourselves." Mary-Ann watched as a bird landed on a low branch of the elm tree in their front yard. "Allan?" she said gently.

"Yes dear."

"Take me somewhere would you." She turned her head and looked longingly into his eyes.

"Take you where?" he asked.

"Somewhere. Anywhere. We've never been out of the city before. It's not too late, is it?"

She turned back to the tree as another bird landed. I wrote a story several years ago about bird watchers. I thought sports were competitive until I watched grown men get into pushing matches for the perfect shot. They were common starlings. Orange beaks, black heads that morphed into peacock colored feathers. Purples, greens and blues melding together. One nestled its head into the neck of the other. I took a shot of Mary-Ann looking at them and thought that might work well for the book cover.

Allan rolled up his sleeves and asked, "Are you unhappy being here?"

"Unhappy? Why would I be unhappy? We have two beautiful children with a third on the way." Mary-Ann paused to rub her belly, her lips stretching across her face into a smile. "We should think of names. I like Carol." She turned again to look at him. Confusion and pain lifted his brow.

"Take me somewhere would you," Mary-Ann said again, rocking gently back and forth. "I will sweetheart. I will." Allan stood, kissed her on the top of the head and walked back into the house.

Stepping out of my car, I slung my bag over my shoulder and walked up to the gate. "Hi, Mary-Ann," I said, pulling on the door. "It's me, Mr. Pitello. From the newspaper." She reached for her walker and started to stand.

"No, please. You don't need to get up. How are you feeling?" I asked at the bottom of the steps.

"I'm doing just fine Mr. Pitello. How's your writing coming along?" she said, as if back in 2008.

"Good. Very good actually. I made it over to Full Bellies not too long ago."

"Oh, did you," she said, sitting up straighter. "We opened in 1953. I still remember the look on Allan's face when I showed him the building. 'Who's going to watch the children while you're working. And who is going to pay to fix this dump?'" Mary-Ann giggled and played with her hair. I walked up and sat on the railing near her, jotting down a few notes as she spoke.

"Took us almost a year to get the place ready, but every month, more and more people offered to help. Tables and chairs were donated by some local churches. Allan's friend Kevin brought his crew over to put in the kitchen, and by that time our paperwork had gone through and we were officially a nonprofit." Mary-Ann's shoulders scrunched into her neck and I could see the joy in her eyes.

"How long has it been since you've visited?" I asked.

Mary-Ann thought for a moment. Her eyes wandered back to the busy street as a car sped by. "Too long."

"Mr. Pitello," Allan said through the screen door. "When did you get here?"

"Just a minute ago. Mary-Ann's been telling me about Full Bellies."

"Oh, has she? God had his hand in all that, 'cause I know it never would have worked otherwise."

Remember Me

Mary-Ann still hadn't gained all of her strength back, which meant she had to use a walker to move about, but she was doing better physically. She leaned an elbow on the arm of the chair and rested her chin in her palm. Allan and I walked down the steps.

"How is she really doing?" I asked.

"Some days are worse than others. Just yesterday she offered to cook something while I was out back working in the garden. I told her not to worry, to just watch her shows and I'd be back in shortly. I was only gone for fifteen minutes. When I came back, she was sitting in the living room watching television, but the entire house smelled of gas. She'd turned the burner on and walked away." Allan rubbed his face with his hands.

"Have you thought of getting help? I know that your sons come by sometimes, but maybe you need to find someone that's a little more permanent."

"I have, but I don't want to choose the wrong person. I don't want Mary-Ann to get it in her head that I'm abandoning her. And she is my wife, my responsibility." He was starting to get agitated, his words getting stuck in his throat.

"But that's why people are hired for those positions. They've been trained for situations like this." I reached out and gently touched his arm.

"You're right. I just feel her slipping away. I can't explain to you how grateful I am that you reached out to us. She's talked more and remember things even I had forgotten just with the conversations she's had with you." Allan reached into his pants pocket and pulled out a folded piece of paper. "I've been talking to some people who have been through this before. A support group, you know. One of them showed me this poem by Owen Darnell and I've been reading it every day." He unfolded the paper and handed it to me.

Do not ask me to remember,
Don't try to make me understand,
Let me rest and know you're with me,
Kiss my cheek and hold my hand.
I'm confused beyond your concept,
I am sad and sick and lost.
All I know is that I need you
To be with me at all cost.
Do not lose your patience with me,
Do not scold or curse or cry.
I can't help the way I'm acting,
Can't be different though I try.
Just remember that I need you,
That the best of me is gone,
Please don't fail to stand beside me,
Love me 'til my life is done.

I folded the paper and handed it back. It took everything in me not to share my tears. "That's beautiful," I said, stepping through the fence.

"I spent a lot of time during the first six months blaming her, blaming me, blaming anything I could. This poem has helped me to look at everything differently." He shook my hand and thanked me for stopping by.

As I drove away, there was one line that I couldn't understand. It was this recurring theme that everyone I spoke with kept running back to and it bothered me. *The best of me is gone.* But she's still here. *The best of me is gone.* But she's in all her children. *The best of me is gone.* But she's in all the people she's made an impact on over the years. *The best of me is gone.* But she's what Full Bellies is all about. *The best of me is gone.*

You should look at the disease through a different lens, I thought to myself. Mary-Ann, Mama, she's everywhere, you've just forgotten how to look.

◇

I had an appointment with Bishop Anderson later that day. The sun peaked out from behind the clouds as I pulled into the church parking lot. Stepping over a small puddle, I walked up a set of steps and in through the side entrance. Red velvet carpets lined the halls. A large welcome desk sat to the left of a door that led into the auditorium. Visitor handouts were piled neatly next to a bowl of mints. Near the door was a small sign that read, *God's House. If you wouldn't put your feet up on the couch at your grandmother's, you shouldn't do it here.* An audible laugh shot through my lips and I shook my head.

"Welcome," a voice said from down the hallway. A heavyset, black woman introduced herself as Donisha and led me up a flight of steps to the offices. "These are some portraits of our previous pastors. This is Pastor Shields," she said, pointed at a black and white photo of a man in a suit. "He founded this church back in 1906. It is one of the last standing black churches in all of Brooklyn."

"Please don't take offense, but why are they still considered *black churches*? Is it taboo for whites to join?"

"Oh, goodness no. We have plenty of white folks in our congregation. I think that because of the way we worship, people assume it's populated primarily by blacks." We continued walking, dim ceiling lights guiding our way around a corner.

"My family were Catholics. No one but the priest spoke. I've been to a few black churches over the years and I had more fun in one two-hour service than I did my entire life in the Catholic church."

Donisha laughed with her entire body and she held her hand over her mouth as if to try and contain it. "See what I mean. We get to shouting and waving our hands and some people think the devil's taken over. That's just the Holy Spirit moving through us." Donisha gave me a hug and told me to sit in the chair outside Bishop Anderson's office. "He should be right out."

The door swung open. I stood, straightening my coat. Bishop Anderson stepped out in a blue, pin striped suit, a white pocket kerchief, and shoes that had recently been shined.

"Good afternoon," he said, shaking my hand.

"Good afternoon. Thank you for taking the time to sit down with me."

"My pleasure." We walked into his office. It smelled of cinnamon and three of the four walls were lined with bookshelves. A circular rug sat under an antique globe. The windows overlooked the city street. His desk glistened, his chairs a polished leather and a large painting of a church on top of a hill hung on the wall behind.

"Have a seat," he said, walking around his desk.

The seat sunk from my weight and I struggled to find a position that didn't make me lean one way or the other. After a moment, I gave up, leaning against the armrest and swinging my leg over my knee. Removing my recorder from my bag, I set it on my lap.

"Before we get into anything specific. I want to know, what's the first thing that comes to mind when I say Mary-Ann Cauldwell."

"Oh man," he said, throwing his hands behind his head. "Mama. There's no other word, feeling, or thought that could come to anybody's mind except, Mama." Bishop Anderson quickly leaned forward, pointing a firm index finger in my direction. "You got a math problem, Mama's got you. You fell off your bike, Mama's got you. You need food for the weekend, Mama's got you. There wasn't anything that woman wouldn't do."

Bishop Anderson was a man in his early-fifties. Maybe two or three years younger than myself, but it's true when they say, 'black don't crack.' If I didn't know any better, I'd have thought he was five years out of theology school. Smooth skin, a trimmed beard without even a hint of grey, arms as big around as my thighs and pair of glasses I swear were only to make him look smarter. And they did, too.

"You've been at this church for…?"

"I grew up in the church, but I've been pastoring for fourteen years and counting. God willing I'll be here for another twenty."

A soft knock came at the door and Donisha walked in carrying a wooden tray with a pitcher of lemonade and two glasses. She set them down on the desk and left.

"That woman right there," he said, pointing at the door. "Is the only reason this church isn't overgrown with dust and falling apart. She keeps a calendar like I keep snacks in my bottom drawer," he said. Laughing, he pulled open the draw and tossed a box of cookies next to the drinks.

"I was told Mary-Ann helped out here as well."

"Until seven, eight years ago she was still spending half of her time here cleaning and running bible study for young women. She was head of the outreach committee, gathering people together to go and share the good news with those who've never heard."

"So what kind of impact would you say she's had on this community?" I asked, pouring a glass of lemonade.

Bishop Anderson let out a sigh. "I can't even put it into words. As a kid, I remember her being the first one to get here. She'd open the church and get things ready before the pastor arrived. And, she'd be the last one to leave, always making sure everyone had everything they needed." He poured a glass of his own and took a drink. A car honked, and I looked out as a woman slammed her hand against the hood. The driver honked again, pressing the gas and speeding away.

"Why did you decide to write this book?" he asked, sitting back in his seat. "Community Woman in Shower Robe Found Four Blocks from Home. That was the headline the Daily Shout used when Mary-Ann was found that day. If you know anything about journalism, a headline can either pull you in, or send you to the sports section." I shrugged my shoulders and set my glass down on his desk.

"I remember that. Made her out to seem crazy, or on some drug spun craze." "And that's exactly what they were trying to do. After reading more, you find out she was a pillar in the neighborhood in the beginning stages of Alzheimer's and Dementia. I knew there was a greater story there, I just wasn't sure how it needed to be told."

"Well I think you're right to speak with the people of the community."

"You're the ones who would know her best."

Bishop Anderson nodded his head slowly, droplets of sweat forming on his brow. He dabbed his head with his kerchief. "What can I help you better understand?" he said, marrying his fingers together in front of his chin.

"I think it's the question every person in the world, especially those who have no faith, ask. Why does God allow something so terrible, so drastic, so painful, to happen to someone who spent their life doing what he asked?"

He sat in silence for a moment, his face pinched in thought. "It's the same reason God allows wonderful things to happen. I know that may sound backwards but think of it like this. Humanity was given free will, the option to choose how they want to live their life. And in that life, someone may choose to harm, or they may choose to do good. Something as simple as a young man holding a door open for an elderly woman could go several different ways. The woman could be grateful, she could chastise the young man saying, 'I don't need your help,' or she could ignore the deed all together. Does that changed the fact that the young man went out of his way to treat the woman kindly and with respect? No, of course not."

"So, God chooses to punish one, reward another, and ignore the last altogether?" I asked, playing devil's advocate.

"I see why you would think of it like that. But, God will never ignore us. We are his creation. Created in his image. He does choose to punish some, 'for all have fallen short of the glory of God,' and our sins must be punished. But those that believe, have their eyes opened to what grace really is."

"And what is that grace? And why and what is Mary-Ann being punished for?"

A smile spread across his face as he answered. "Grace is a gift. But a gift that is undeserved. A gift of unconditional love." He paused to stand. Looking out the window he said, "I can't speak for God. He may be punishing Mary-Ann for something she did, or possibly something someone else did. But it's because he knows that she can handle it. It's being done for his glory, that we as a community can stand together and worship him for all he has done for us."

Bishop Anderson turned around and walked to the globe. "When I first found out, I was angry. Angry at God for the same reason we all get angry. Lack of understanding. But when I thought on it, when I prayed on it, I realized something. How many people have the opportunity to be remembered while they're still alive?" That question froze me in my tracks. My eyes darted up and he could tell that he had struck a nerve.

"Exactly," he said, pointing a finger. "As painful as this is for her family and this community, we aren't waiting for her to go before we remember all she's done. Four months ago, Donisha came to me with an idea. To put a memory box in the back of the sanctuary. To challenge the congregation to write down something they remember Mama doing for them or their family and drop it in the box on their way out. Ask me how many times that box has been filled," he said, excitement building in his voice.

"How many?" I asked, genuinely matching his excitement.

He shrugged his blazer off and walked back to his seat, draping it over the back. "Every week for four months. When Donisha and I sat down and talked about it, we thought we might get enough to put a collage together to share with the family. We had to dedicate half of one our Sunday School rooms for the papers alone." Bishop Anderson sat down with a loud thud, his head dotted with sweat and his breathing heavy.

I almost couldn't believe it. *The best of me is gone,* still rang in the back of my mind, but I realized this was the proof I needed to help Allan and his family and some still in the community, to look at this situation through a different lens.

Bishop Anderson offered to show me the room. Scriptures lined the walls. Stacks of chairs were pushed to the side waiting for Sunday morning. The far side of the room had three tables in a row covered in boxes. Each box overflowed with folded pieces of paper. I reached in and unfolded one. *When my child was hungry, you brought me to Full Bellies to get a meal.* Placing it back in, I grabbed another. *My husband lost his job at the factory and you brought us a meal and prayed outside our home. A week later, my husband got a job at the post office.*

"They're all like this?" I asked, setting the second paper back in the box. Bishop Anderson could do nothing but smile and shake his head.

◇

Months later, I stood in the thick summer air, my shirt sticking to my skin. Beads of sweat poked through like daggers making it look as though I had just finished a half-marathon. Ducking under a tree, I watched as a small crowd hurried through the doors of the church. Allan and Mary-Ann were unaware, but that Sunday would be all about them.

Aaron pulled up and I opened the door for Mary-Ann, helping her onto the sidewalk. She wore a vibrant yellow dress with white and black accents on the sleeves. A floppy hat rested gracefully on her head and her neck was covered in pearls.

"Good morning," I said.

"Mr. Pitello," she replied with a wink.

Allan stepped out of the car in an auburn suit and black tie with silver cufflinks pinned to his wrists.

"Where's your walker?" I asked, looking in the back seat.

"He just got out of the car," Mary-Ann said with a laugh, wrapping her gloved hands around Allan's forearm. Allan smiled and shrugged his shoulders as if knowing he had no choice.

Just inside the front door were dozens of letters hanging from a wire that led into the sanctuary. Allan paused as he read the first. "What is all of this?" he asked, looking back at me.

"They did this for the two of you," I said, pointed to the wire.

Donisha stood by the visitors table holding a stack of bulletins. She was wearing a dark, violet dress and her smile cascaded boldly from her lips.

"Allan. Mary-Ann," she said, stepping forward. "I'm happy to welcome you to what Helping Hands Baptist Church will forever know as Cauldwell Sunday. If you would follow me, we have your seats reserved." Donisha slowly opened the door and led them into the sanctuary.

As they entered, the sound of hundreds of people standing thundered throughout the room. All along the walls and hanging from the rafters were the letters the church had collected over the months. A large sign at the front of the church read, *We Love You, Mama,* and the choir, dressed in full robes swayed gently back and forth as they hummed the melody to *Blessed Assurance.* Their journey to the front was slow, collecting hugs, handshakes and smiles along the way. As the congregation sat, and the choir fell silent, Bishop Anderson walked up on stage. He removed a light grey jacket and placed it over the arm of a chair.

"Blessed morning," he said, his voice like a crashing wave. "I want to thank you all for coming out to this special occasion." Wiping his face with a towel, he leaned forward, resting his arm on the pulpit. "Don't get things twisted, we are not here to worship these two. We are here to celebrate the fact that God has placed them in our lives."

"Amen," a woman shouted.

"As you can see, there are hundreds of slips of paper all around this room. They are reminders of how the Cauldwell's used their gifts from God, to share love and bring joy to each and every one of you."

"Thank you, Jesus," another said, waving their hand through the air.

Bishop Anderson walked down the steps and helped Mary-Ann to her feet. "We took up an offering last Sunday and asked that if God placed the burden on their heart to give boldly to you and your family, then instead of running from that burden, they run headlong into that burden with God leading the way." He removed a small envelope from his pocket and handed it to Mary-Ann.

"This is one way we would like to thank you for being a leader, a friend, a comforter and a mother in our community," he said as the congregation began to clap.

Mary-Ann held the envelope to her chest and began to cry, saying, 'thank you,' her voice lost in the applause. Bishop Anderson raised a hand to quiet the crowd. Allan helped Mary-Ann back to her seat and put his arm around her shoulder.

"We would also like to share this video with you." Bishop Anderson walked back on stage. "Because of Donisha's hard work, we were able to gather together photographs and personal testimonies of how you've impacted the lives of those in our community."

One of the deacons used a hand crank to lower a white screen. The lights dimmed as the video began. *We love you Mary-Ann*, said a group of teens standing under a tree. The screen flashed to a picture of Mary-Ann holding a baby in each arm as she stood at the front of a room teaching a bible study. Her hair was cut short and bobby pinned away from her face. Next was a short video of her in her early forties chasing a group of teens with a water balloon. The crowd roared with laughter.

The video flashed with testimonies of women finding shelter in the Cauldwell home, men learning how to tie a tie from Allan before they went to a job interview, and old friends sharing stories of her as a child.

Tears mixed with laughter, and laughter blended gracefully with shouts of adoration. As the video came to a close, the last scene was of Sharice. She sat in her wheelchair, arms resting in her lap. She wore a pair of sunglasses to hide her eye, but the way her mouth twitched, I could only imagine she was hiding her tears as well.

Hey meatball, she said. Her head tilted to the side and a gentle smile slid across her lips. *I saw a rainbow the other day and thought of when we used to dream about the pot of gold waiting on the other side. I miss sitting in my mama's house painting nails. Or standing on those blocks getting our hands dirty in the flour as we baked cookies. I miss trying on dresses before school and giggling when a boy looked our way. I miss tearing down those walls and cleaning the floor to the soup kitchen we built together, and the look on your Allan's face as you walked down the aisle. The way you held and loved each of your children, the same way you held and loved my own. But the past is there to remember. And the here and now, well, it's here to hold onto until it becomes the past. I love you sister.*

Her video faded to a picture of them standing outside Full Bellies, arms wrapped around each other's shoulders, cheeks squished together, eyes closed and mouths wide open in the purest smile.

A thunderous applause rang out as the lights flickered, returning the room to a bright glow. Bishop Anderson stood smiling, looking down at Allan and Mary-Ann.

"Stand with me and worship," he said, turning over his shoulder and nodding to the choir.

We sang for what seemed hours, a line of people filling the middle aisle dancing, waving towels in the air. As the music settled and the people sat, Bishop Anderson spoke of new beginnings. Taking what is old, what is broken, what is weighing you down, and casting it away, allowing God to set forth a new path.

The service ended, and the wires were cut, letting the notes fall like snowflakes to the sanctuary floor. I helped Donisha and a few others collect and place them in a box for Mary-Ann to bring home.

"You were a part of this?" Allan asked as we walked downstairs to where refreshments were being served. Nodding, I opened the door. A cool breeze pushed through each layer of clothing like cold water being poured on my head. Shivering, I welcomed it with a smile.

"Thank you," he said, placing a hand on my shoulder.

"I thought it would only be appropriate to let her see how much she's loved, you know, before she forgets." We walked to a small table where Mary-Ann was already sitting. A few of the women from the soup kitchen were there, along with Aaron. Tears still trickled from Mary-Ann's eyes, getting caught in the corner of her lips as she smiled.

"That was so lovely Allan, wasn't it? They've named a day after us," she said, taking a napkin and wiping her nose.

"I know sweetheart. It's unbelievable." He took the seat beside her and I walked to a table to get a glass of water.

"Donisha," I said, tapping her arm. She turned and greeted me with a hug. "It turned out really well don't you think?"

"Absolutely. I couldn't have imagined it any better." She handed me a cup.

"Mary-Ann will love reading through those letters." I agreed, thanked her again for letting me be a part of it, and walked back to where the Cauldwell's were seated.

"Can I read one of the notes to you?" I asked, taking a slip of paper out of my pocket. "I was hoping you might remember and could elaborate."

"Sure. I don't see why not," Mary-Ann said.

Unfolding the paper, I read, *you sold your car in the spring of 1959, so I could pay for college.*

I didn't find out until ten years later, but I promise I would not be where I am today if not for you. Thank you, Mama.

"You sold your car?" I said, tossing the paper on the table. Mary-Ann's lip curled, and she looked over at Allan who was hiding behind his hands.

"Why don't you ask the person whose idea it was?"

"Allan?" I said, turning in my seat.

"Now don't go making this all about me," he complained, leaning his cane against the table. "Yes, it was my idea, but it was Mary-Ann who did all the haggling with the dealership." Embarrassed, he turned the story back to her.

"Anthony Walters. One of the smartest, young African Americans I'd seen. If one of our daughters would have had their wits about them, they could have had themselves a fine husband." She turned and sniffed her nose in the air. Allan chuckled, leaning back in his chair and exhaling audibly.

"His mother had gotten sick and passed away when he was a boy, and his father worked hard to keep him in school. But when graduation rolled around, he was going to have to give it all up to find a job." Mary-Ann reached over and gripped Allan's wrist. "Allan came home one day fittin and frettin about a conversation he'd overheard. Said

God was tugging on his heart to do something about it. The next morning, he sent me down to the dealership to work something out with the salesman. A week later, Allan dropped an envelope in their mailbox with a letter that said, 'For Anthony to go to school."

"I had no idea that's what happened to the car," Aaron said, his mouth falling open. "This whole time I thought you'd just gotten sick of it. Never in a million years did I think you sold it to send someone to college."

Mary-Ann smiled, folding her arms over her lap. "This life isn't about boasting in all you've done. It's about sitting back and letting God get the glory."

"Well, I think God is sharing a bit of that glory with you today," I said. "Will you read them?" I asked.

"Certainly. How else will I find out who forgot to thank me," she said, rolling with laughter. "As much as he doesn't want to admit it, Allan was a much bigger part in this than you know. So, I look forward to reading them and being reminded of what he's done."

Just then, Bishop Anderson walked to the table. Leaning down, he planted a soft kiss on Mary-Ann's cheek, then turned and shook Allan's hand firmly. "What a wonderful day," he said, itching at his collar.

"Indeed, it is," Allan said. "Thank you, and your team for putting it all together."

"Absolutely. It's well deserved." He placed a firm hand on my shoulder and said, "And make sure you keep this guy around. He's a good one." Those at the table nodded in agreement, sending heat back to my neck and cheeks. The crowd dwindled as the afternoon pressed on, hands by the dozen coming by to give Mary-Ann and Allan hugs, thanking them again for all they'd done.

Chapter 5

November 4, 2008

"Who did you vote for?" Aaron asked. We were all crammed into Allan's living room and I felt like a kid who had come home for a university holiday. Aaron and Prince sat in the reclining chairs. Allan sat next to Mary-Ann, who was, like always, wrapped in a quilted blanket. I was on the floor leaning against the coffee table. Carol, who had arrived only a few days ago from Florida, sat on the other side of the coffee table, her back resting against the arm of the love seat.

It had been months since I visited. The obvious reason being the presidential race and the potential of our country electing its first African American president. I should have been anywhere but there that night. The office, DC, my condo drinking a beer with my dog, anticipating the eruption New York City would make if Obama was elected. But I chose to be in that quaint, loving home with the Cauldwell family.

"Is there a right answer to that question?" I said, looking back at Aaron. Prince laughed, tossing peanuts in the air and catching them in his mouth.

"You better not go making a mess over there," Mary-Ann said.

"Yes, Mama," Prince said, looking around his seat to find the one he'd just dropped. "What do you mean?" Aaron burst. "Of course, there's a right answer to that question." "Ha. It's not that simple. If I say John McCain, what does that make me?" I asked, reaching forward for my beer.

"A racist," Carol said with a laugh.

"Exactly," I said, thankful I hadn't taking a drink yet or it would have been sprayed across the floor.

"No. I wouldn't call you a racist. I'd just say you were, *misunderstood*," he finished.

My face twisted. "Misunderstood? Come on now. I've lived in New York City my entire life. I know black culture."

"Leave the man alone," Allan stuck in, patting me on the head like a defeated child. "Ah, who am kidding. I'd call you a racist myself." The room roared with laughter. Carol fell onto her side and slammed her hand against the ground and

Prince began to cough, having swallowed a few peanuts before chewing.

Carol slid her feet up under her thighs and said, "If you're so knowledgeable, name five iconic black figures whose names aren't, Malcolm X, Dr. Martin Luther King Jr., Harriet Tubman, or Muhammed Ali." She crossed her arms and pursed her lips.

"That's easy. Nelson Mandela. He spent over twenty years in a South African prison to then be elected as president. And doesn't it seem odd that a country stricken with apartheid into the 90s elected a black president before the United States of America?" I looked around the room at stunned faces.

Prince spoke to break the silence. "Yeah, but it's Africa. There's more black people there to choose from," he said sarcastically.

"Number two," I continued, pushing my sleeves up to my elbows. "Frederick Douglas. Former slave turned leader in the anti-slavery movement. Three, and this one *you* might not even know. Toussaint Louverture. In 1791, he led a successful Haitian slave revolt that eventually led to a plantation system with paid labor. Four. Jesse Owens. Four gold medal wins in the 1936 Olympics. Hitler's Olympics, to be more specific." I paused to take a drink and saw smiles on each and every one of their faces.

"Can't think of a fifth one, can you?" Aaron said.

"Hold on a second. I could do this for hours. Number five. Michael Jackson. Pioneer in the music indust—"

"Wait a minute now," Mary-Ann said suddenly. Her face was pinched in confusion. "I thought they said five *black* figures." Mary-Ann winked.

If you've ever been around a black family, they love to talk, and they love to laugh. Words can't explain the number of tears that fell from each of our faces after that statement, but I imagine we could have filled an ocean. Several long minutes of catching our breath took place before anyone could talk, our sides aching with joy.

"I'll do you one better, Mama," I said, not realizing what I had called her.

"Took you long enough," Mary-Ann said, stuffing her blanket back under her legs and smiling. Whatever it was about her, it had finally taken over.

"I realize I didn't put any women on that list, so I'll give you two. Maya Angelou, inspiring American poet and writer. And, Deratu Tulu. The first Ethiopian female athlete to win Olympic gold."

"Thank you," she said, clasping her hands together. "I approve."

"He's got my vote," Allan said swiftly.

"Mine too," said Prince.

Carol and Aaron looked at each other, their heads twisting to the side. "Okay, you proved that you know your black history Sal, but just because you know black culture, doesn't mean you know what it means to be black," Aaron said.

"Now that's an entirely different topic. I'm a middle-aged, bald, Italian white guy with no wife, no kids, and dog. I've lived in Brooklyn most of my life and I've been writing for a newspaper for almost thirty years. Of course, I don't know what it means to be black. But I love everything about culture in general and respect the efforts of a lot of black people in history, as well as the present." Aaron scrunched his face.

"Come on, give me a break," I said, waving my arms. "I'm sitting in the living room of a black family. Just behind me is someone who could easily be on that list of black figures who helped to change the course of history. And, we're watching the countdown to a potential first African American president." I paused to point at him. "Who by the way, I voted for."

Aaron laughed, throwing a small handful of peanuts at me. "If I didn't know any better I'd say you *were* black. That's all you had to say in the first place and this conversation would have been over but leave it to a black person to come up with a reason to argue."

After brushing the peanuts off my arm, I looked back at him and said, "In all my years, that's the nicest thing anyone has ever said to me." The room roared again. A few more handfuls of peanuts were thrown in different directions and I nearly spilled my beer.

As we settled, the house gently fell to a low murmur, only the sound of the television and the occasional slurp of a drink could be heard. Allan flipped back and forth between stations several times before leaving it on NBC. I explained that no matter what news station you went to, it would essentially be the same information, you just had to choose which person's voice you enjoyed listening to most. By nine o'clock, Allan and Mary-Ann were asleep, their heads leaning in against one another. Carol had dozed several times before heading upstairs for the night. Prince, Aaron and I sat focused as Obama's number's continued to rise.

"I think he's got it," I whispered, finishing of the last of my third beer.

"I wouldn't say that yet," Aaron said. "There are still a few states that could make the difference for McCain."

The next few hours pressed on and Obama's lead looked to be too much. *This just in*, Tim Russert, NBC Nightly News reporter said. *McCain has just given his concession speech at the Baltimore Hotel in Phoenix. Barack Obama has won the presidency.* Aaron stood and raised his arms high above his head. His mouth fell open in a whispered shout and he and his brother hugged with excitement.

"This is a special moment," I whispered, standing to join them. We all looked back at Allan and Mary-Ann, their breath rising and falling in perfect union. Most people go through life not reaping, or even seeing the benefits of their sacrifice. I was glad to know that they would.

With the hour that it was, Aaron offered to let me sleep in the guest room. I happily accepted. As I lay on the bed, arms folded over my chest, I thought of my dad. We weren't close until I reached my mid-thirties and he was diagnosed for the first time. I fell asleep with something he had said replaying in my mind. *Be proud of what you can do, not what others can do for you.*

◇

"We'll be taking my mother to Full Bellies this evening for dinner and to celebrate the election," Prince said, standing in the kitchen drinking coffee.

I poured a mug for myself. "I have an early dinner with my brother Mike after I leave the office, but I'll stop by on my way home." After saying goodbye, I stopped at home to thank my neighbors for looking after Scout. Tossing him a treat, I made sure his water was full, then headed to the office.

"It's a mad world out there," I said as I walked in. Ryan was sitting at his desk scrolling through second drafts. Domonique, our photographer, flipped through her camera examining photos she had taken the night before. Robert, our staff intern, was eating a donut, eyes glued to the small television hanging on the wall.

"It's as if aliens from another planet just landed. This is insane," Robert said, turning to face me, a thin smear of powdered sugar on his cheek.

"I can't say they would have made this much of a fuss if aliens were actually here," Domonique said, looking up from her camera. "I've seen rioting when things are going badly but rioting out of joy. That just doesn't make any sense. I've got hundreds of photos. Cars flipped over and set on fire. Store-front windows smashed in with people carrying out electronics. All the while, shouting how happy they are that a black man was elected president." She rolled her chair over to where I was standing to show me.

"I heard on the bus radio this morning that it's no different on the other side of the country," I said.

"Just add that to the list of things to write about," Ryan said. He stood and walked over to the printer, then placed the papers on a desk.

"Who was in DC covering the story last night?" I asked.

"Peter was at the white house. He sent me a draft last night," Ryan said, pointing at the desk he had just walked from. "Amy took a crew down for live, online coverage."

"Of course, she would," I said with a laugh.

Amy was an incredible journalist. She won the Peabody Award ten years ago for her work on *Saving Lives: The real story behind sex slavery in America.* But it wasn't often that the chief of staff did work in the field. That's why I never wanted the promotion. I needed to be out there gathering information to tell the story, not making sure other people were telling it correctly.

"This is a big event," Ryan said.

"I would have done the same thing in her position," Robert said, wiping his face with a napkin. "I was told to stay in the office in case something crazy happens." He shook his head. "All the crazy stuff is happening out there!"

"Calm down, Intern. It's not like something like this will never happen again," Domonique said, smirking. "Oh, that's right, it won't." Robert's face reddened and the rest of us turned away and laughed.

"Alright, let's leave the poor kid alone. Ryan, email me the story on water shortages, I want to look back over that before we go to print. When

I'm done I'll take the train into Manhattan and take some shots of the aftermath." I checked my watch. "It's nine forty-five now. Dom, are you good with taking Robert into the city? I'd like some interviews with people of every race, age, sex, size, sexual orientation. You name it. I want to know how the people feel after the election."

"Hell yes!" Robert shouted.

"He asked me if I was okay with taking you with me. I haven't answered yet." Domonique ran her fingers through her hair. Robert's mouth hung open slightly and he pleaded with his eyes. "Fine, I'll take you, but act like a normal person, would you?"

"Once I leave the office, I won't be coming back until Monday. If you need anything, you'll have to reach me on my cell."

"Look at you, Sal," Ryan said sarcastically. "We get you a computer and now you're saying, 'reach me on my *cell.*' I think we've created a monster." I walked away shaking my head.

Several hours later I stood in the middle of Manhattan, camera slung over my right shoulder as thousands of people walked the streets shouting, crying and hugging one another. Chants of U.S.A. went on for minutes at a time. Children sat on top of shoulders, gripping the heads of their fathers. Hundreds of police in riot gear lined the sidewalks in hopes of containing any madness that might ensue. I found my way to a staircase to take pictures. A cool fall breeze rushed through the air, carrying the words of the crowd even further into the city.

By ten-thirty, the screens on the sides of the buildings all went to a recording of Obama's victory speech in Chicago. He wore a black suit, white shirt and red tie, his hand gripping that of his youngest daughter as they waved to the people. The crowd fell to a gentle hum as he started to speak.

If there is anyone out there who still doubts that America is a place where all things are possible, who still wonders if the dream of our founders is alive in our time, who still questions the power of our democracy,   tonight, is your answer.

The Manhattan crowd exploded, throwing balls of newspaper into the air. Pumping their fists, they chanted as if they were fans watching a USA World Cup game. Several police horses stumbled away, one nearly throwing its riders to the ground.

There's something special about seeing a nation come together, or at least a people putting aside their differences to welcome a new way of thinking. Like the freeing of the slaves, the end of World War ll, and a woman's right to vote; history was being made.

◇

The line to get into Full Bellies extended a block and a half. I acted as press coverage, walking along the cracked and aging sidewalk to the front door. Slowly making my way through, I ran into Katrina, who landed a rather aggressive hug around my neck.

"It's great to see you, Mr. Pitello," she said, pushing the door open and walking me in.

"You too," I said with a smile.

Decorations hung from the ceiling, dim lights lined the outer edges of the wall and most of the tables and chairs were folded and stacked against the wall to make more room. Music thumped in the background, muffled by all the talking. I saw Prince by the drink counter talking with a woman while filling cups. "Prince. This was a great turn out," I said, resting my arms on the counter.

"Yeah, and I'm told there are a lot more still outside," he said, handing me a cup. I shook my head in agreement, looking over at the woman.

"Oh, Sal," Prince said, grabbing her by the arm. "This is my wife Elizabeth." She had a part down the middle of her head, thin bangs hanging down to her glasses and a slightly crooked smile. But it was the pale skin, like me, that separated her from many others.

"I've heard a lot about you, Sal," she said. "I think it's nice what you're doing for Mary-Ann and the family.

Smiling, I took sip of water and set my cup down. "Where's your mother? I'd like to see her," I said, turning my attention back to Prince.

"The last time I saw her she was sitting along the wall with Sharice." He pointed through the crowd. I nodded, working my way through a mob of people wearing Obama 2008 party hats and snacking on cheese and crackers. Mary-Ann sat in a metal folding chair next to Sharice, her wheelchair locked and pressed against the wall. Sharice was telling a story. I stood at a distance watching Mary-Ann's facial expressions change, her mouth stretching into her famous smile.

"Ladies," I said, approaching with my hand extended.

Sharice looked up. "If you've come over here like that you better be asking one of us to dance." She cracked a smile and looked over at Mary-Ann.

"You better stop that, Sharice," Mary-Ann said, gripping her hand. "He's a nice-looking man but I don't think Ronald would appreciate you flirting with another man." Mary-Ann blushed, smiling up at me.

"Who are you anyway?" she asked. Sharice's expression sank into her chin. "Don't you remem—"

I held my hand out, pausing her mid-sentence. "My name is Sal Pitello. I'm here writing a story about you and your family."

Mary-Ann scrunched her nose, looking around the room. "Why would anyone want to do that?" she asked.

"I think your story is worth telling. You've done a lot for this community and I think people should know about it." I walked to the other side of Mary-Ann and sat.

"Isn't that nice," she said. "I couldn't have done it without this woman right here. She's my best friend, Sha... She... Umm." She looked back at Sharice, her head tilting to the side. "Sharice. Yes, this is my best friend Sharice. We got all this started, ah, when was it honey?"

"Many years ago," Sharice said. She looked past Mary-Ann, locking eyes with me and I could see how much it hurt.

"Yes, so many years ago," Mary-Ann said. Her eyes wandered back to the crowd. "My, there's a lot of people here. I wonder why that is."

I pulled my phone from pocket and pulled up the headline news. "We are celebrating. Barack Obama became the forty-fourth president." I turned my screen to show her a picture.

"Oh, good heavens. Never did I think I'd see a black president," she said. Her face lit up and she took my phone to get a closer look. "Handsome too," she giggled. "Did you see this?" she asked, spinning back to Sharice.

"Yes. It's a special time in our country. That's why we wanted to bring everyone down to celebrate. It goes to show that the hard work we put in for equality is starting to pay off."

"Celebrating. Sorry, I've forgotten. What are we celebrating?" Mary-Ann said, looking down at the phone. "I don't know who this is, but he sure is handsome. Don't go telling Al I've been having eyes at another man." She giggled again, setting the phone down on her leg.

With a saddened smile, Sharice stroked Mary-Ann's cheek with the back of her hand, tears scattering slowly across her face. "I won't, honey. I know Allan is the only man for you."

I watched for a few short minutes. Sharice began to hum as she looked into Mary-Ann's eyes. Mary-Ann smiled back, and I could see the love they shared for one another. The music grew louder, and clusters of people began to dance, raising their cups in the air and shouting with excitement.

Alise came over shortly after. "I think it would be best if you took a break from all this noise, Mother." Sharice nodded her head, lifting her legs back onto the footholds. "Mr. Pitello, will you help Mama to the office?"

"Of course," I said. Grabbing my phone and standing, I held out my wrist.

"What is it you want me to do? I hope you aren't looking for a dance, I've got a husband, you know," Mary-Ann said, leaning back in her chair. I chuckled. "I would do no such thing, Mama. If you hold onto my arm, I'll help you walk back to the office and away from all this noise." She hesitated, then slowly grabbed my arm and I led her through the dancing crowd.

As we walked through the door, Aaron, his wife Andrea, Carol and Sharice were sitting around a small table looking through a box of old photographs. After helping Mary-Ann into a seat, I introduced myself to Andrea and found a seat of my own.

"Who is this?" Andrea asked, holding up a black and white photo of a young boy.

"There's nothing written on the back." His hair was trimmed short and head tilted slightly to the right. He was wearing torn overalls, one strap unhooked and a white Long John shirt with the sleeves rolled to his elbows.

Sharice leaned forward against the table and laughed. "Who else do we know that wore overalls every day to work? And still wears those things to this day?" The room looked at one another and all at once said, "Allan."

"Yeah?" Allan said from the doorway. "I knew I felt my ears burning." Andrea held the photograph up for him to see.

"Ah. I see you found me in my prime. Handsome little fellow, wasn't I?" Allan walked forward and hung his arms over Mary-Ann's shoulders, kissing her gently on the head.

Mary-Ann spun quickly, knocking Allan back. "Who do you think you are? I have a husband!" she shouted, throwing her arms in the air.

Allan looked around the room embarrassed. "It's me, love. Allan," he said, waddling forward with his cane.

Mary-Ann reached up and took his face in her hands. Her eyes began to swell. "There you are. I've been waiting for you all night." She kissed him on the cheek. "There was a bald white man who tried to dance with me. Can you believe how many people are here?"

"I know. They're here for you and to celebrate history being made," he said, pulling the chair out next to her and taking a seat.

"Who's here for me?" she asked. "The house is a mess. I should clean up before they arrive, maybe bake a cake. It's their birthday, isn't it?" Suddenly frantic, she tried to stand. Allan took her arm and she sank back into her seat.

"It will be fine. Let's just sit here and look at some pictures."

"Look here Mary-Ann. This is from our tenth-grade dance. Do you remember?" Sharice said, pointing at the picture. "We were sitting at the lunch table and Eugene Yurps and his big head kept looking over at you. You asked me to go with you so that if he asked, you could say you already had a date."

Mary-Ann's eyes went back and forth from the photo to Sharice as if trying to find the connection.

"You were so beautiful in that dress," Sharice said, picking up the photo and holding it close to her face.

"Yes, she was," Allan said, rubbing Mary-Ann's back. "Just as beautiful as she is today." He leaned in and nestled his face in her neck. Mary-Ann giggled, twisting away.

"Take me somewhere," Mary-Ann whispered. Allan kissed her again, whispering something in her ear that made her smile. Turning back to the table, he too thumbed through a stack of photographs as a tear fell from his eye.

Chapter 6

Christmas 2008

My plane landed. I grabbed my bags and headed through the terminal. I wasn't sure how many of the five children were going to be there, my sister liked to surprise me.

Uncles aren't supposed to play favorites, but her eldest and only boy, Grayson, was mine. I used to call him *fathead* when he was barely old enough to speak. That evolved into 'Angela, you've seen how big his teeth are right?" To which I'd suffer a backhanded blow to the arm and laughter would soon follow.

As I stepped on the escalator, a sign reading, *Weclome to Forida Unlce Sal*, was being held in front of four pairs of little feet, the ribbons in their hair just barely peeking over the top. As a writer, I wanted to scream, but as an uncle, it was the cutest thing I had ever seen.

"All five huh?" I said as I gave my sister a hug.

"Harvey's at work and the only one that can stay home by himself wanted to come," she said, squeezing my cheeks like the mother she is.

"Where did my little fathead go," I said, pulling Grayson in for a hug. "You're almost as tall as I am."

"That's not saying much," he jeered.

"Hey now. I still have some embarrassing pictures of you I can gladly show your little girlfriends."

"I don't have any girlfriends," he said.

"Ah, but one day you will, so remember that."

After handing Grayson one of my bags, I knelt down to get smothered with kisses and hugs from my four nieces; Kristi, Paula, Vivian, and Margo. "I've missed you all so much," I said, my voice muffled through their arms.

"We missed you too," they said.

My face was covered in different colored lipstick and glitter, but it was the most relaxed I'd felt in weeks.

"Now, your uncle is here for work too, so he's not going to be able to spend every waking moment with you," Angela said as she herded the girls outside, across the street and into their waiting van.

Grayson and I walked several feet behind chatting about sports and that he was planning on learning to surf.

"I'm surprised you haven't learned already. You do live thirty seconds from the beach."

Grayson stuffed my bags into the back and whispered, "Yeah but mom was afraid of everything. 'What if I bump my head and drown?' 'What if I get eaten by a shark?'" He shook his head in frustration. I couldn't help but laugh. It sounded exactly like my sister.

The forty-minute car ride back to their beach house was filled with loud singing and laughter, the girls encouraging me to 'let loose and dance.'

"Can you take the girls to the back-patio Grayson? Your uncle and I will meet you there," Angela said as we walked into the house. "And don't let any of them go down to the water until we are outside."

"Yes mom," he said, running to his room to change.

Angela poured two glasses of wine and we sat it in the kitchen. "What's been going on?" she asked, sliding a glass over. "I feel like when you come down is the only time I get to really talk to you."

"Well, you have a family. And my life isn't exactly that exciting." I swirled the wine in the glass before having a taste, pretending to be a connoisseur.

"Our lives aren't that much different when you think about it. You probably wake up, feed your dog, read the news, go into your office, write the news, eat lunch, chat with coworkers, go to the bar, head home and do it all over again." She laughed, taking a sip of her wine. "My life is the same, you just need to replace children and husband with a few of those. And the occasional basketball game or dance recital." Understanding her logic, I nodded my head.

"You know, for a man of words, you don't say much."

"I've been that way my entire life. That's why I write. It gives me an opportunity to think about what I want to say rather than just spewing every thought from my mouth."

"So, what you're saying is, I spew?" she said, bursting with laughter. "Okay, you're totally right. But most Italian women do."

"Which is why Harvey must love you so much. You aren't afraid to say what's on your mind." I took another sip of wine, then set the glass down and arched my back.

"So what stories are you working on right now?" she asked.

"Nothing too exciting down here, but I'm actually working on a novel."

Angela swung her arm across the table and hit me. "What the heck, Sal? That's the kind of thing I want to hear about."

"Sorry," I said, rubbing my arm. "It's still in the beginning stages. But, it's about a woman with Alzheimer's and the struggle she and her family have as she deteriorates." I stood and walked to the back door, looking out at the ocean. "She's one of the most loving and loved women I've ever met. The community calls her Mama."

Angela slammed her palm on the kitchen table. "It's about a real person? I thought you were making the story up as you went along."

"No, I read an article about her a while back. There was something that drew me in. I guess I was thinking about how terrible it would be to forget my family or watch someone I loved forget me."

Angela wrapped her arms around my waist and squeezed, planting a kiss on my already colorful cheek. "That's why you need a wife. I get worried with you all alone in that city."

"Well," I started, looking down at her with a smirk. She pulled away and hit me again, this time even harder.

"I swear it's nothing even close to serious at the moment. We just get along really well." Before she could hit me a third time, I pushed open the door and ran down the steps. Moments later, Angela brought me another glass of wine and we sat in the sun, watching the girls play in the sand.

◇

"Allan, how are you?" I said, sitting on the back porch looking through my notes.

"Fine. And yourself?" he asked.

"I'm wonderful actually. Enjoying the beautiful Florida weather and spending some time with my sister's family."

"That's good, that's good. I'm just calling to give you an update on Mary-Ann. I know you said you'd be gone for what, four months?"

I swung my feet off the railing and sat up, flipping my notebook to the next page. "Just under four months. I'm a guest writer down here during the winter and I'm doing a piece on sinkholes and the increase in erosion."

"Right, right. Well, Mary-Ann's doing okay. She struggles to eat most days but we're trying."

"But she has to eat Allan," I said with a hint of frustration.

"Right. She gets lost sometimes, doesn't recognize the house and it scares her. And I can't force the food down her throat."

I made a note to contact Aaron, then stood and walked down to the beach. "I'll let you go. I just wanted you to know how things were going," Allan said.

"Thank you. Make sure she eats something today alright and get some rest. You sound exhausted."

The sand was cool between my toes as I sat on a small hump. A few joggers passed by and waved. A dog jumped into the water to retrieve a frisbee. I looked out at the crashing waves where Cape Romano's *Dome Houses* now stood in almost five feet of water. Over a thirty-year period, the beach receded two-hundred feet. Florida's southern coast was getting smaller and smaller each year. After taking a mental picture, I walked back to the house to change.

◇

Lights blinked on and off around the house as the girls finished painting their bulb ornaments, a Christmas Eve tradition we started when Grayson was six. I hung my arm over the back of Vivian's chair, leaning in to inspect her work.

"That looks beautiful," I said, nestling my chin in her neck.

"What about mine?" Paula asked, holding a golf ball size ornament in the air and shedding a three-toothed smile.

Remember Me

I held my hands over my lips, letting my eyes grow wide. "That should be in a museum under a glass box it's so wonderful." She smiled the way little girls do when they think anything is possible. Setting the ornament down on her area of newspaper, she hopped off her seat and walked to the kitchen sink.

"Let me help you with that," Angela said, sliding a box under Paula's feet and squeezing soap into her hands. "You've all got about ten minutes before we're going to open one present before bed."

I watched as Grayson eyed the tree. There were almost as many presents as there were lights. Some piled high and others leaning against the wall. Harvey sat in a large reclining chair in the living room working away on his laptop, the weather channel playing softly in the background. He was a financial advisor for a large pharmaceutical company and traveled six months out of the year. And the days he was home, Angela told me, were as if he wasn't there. I certainly respected the man. Tall, handsome, a Columbia University graduate, a provider for people who share the same blood as me. But, coming from an Italian family where we would have dinner at our grandmother's house every Sunday; family is the most important thing in this world.

"Alright, everyone find your seats," Angela said, herding the girls into the living room. "Come here sweetheart," Harvey said, closing his computer and setting it on the coffee table. Paula, in her purple onesie, hopped into her father's lap clutching a stuffed elephant in her hands.

I sat on the floor with Vivian snuggled under my arm. Kristi and Margo, the twins, sat under a blanket beside their mother on the couch; and Grayson stood next to the tree. Being the oldest, he was the designated gift finder.

"We want to open ours together," the twins said, their pigtails flipping from one side to the other. The only way I can tell them apart was the scar just above Margo's eye from when she fell off her bed.

"Paula's first, she's the youngest," Grayson said, reaching down to find a present with her name on it. "Here you go."

"Now that's a cute little purse," Harvey said, tossing the wrapping paper on the ground. Paula looked up at him and smiled. Kristi and Margo opened their gift from me. Matching sunglasses. The face they made when they put them on said that I hadn't done a half-bad job. I helped Vivian open hers, a rather heavy box filled with crafts to make jewelry, and by the time we were done, she had already constructed a bracelet and matching ring.

Grayson rolled up the sleeves of his shirt as he sat on the edge of the coffee table. "I know what this is," he said, holding a thin present in his hand.

"Oh yeah?" Angela said, raising her eyebrows.

"It's an Xbox game." Grayson shook the gift gently by his ear.

"How could it be an Xbox game if you don't even have an Xbox?" she said.

"Well, if it is a game, then there must be an Xbox in there somewhere."

"Open it already," Vivian shouted.

"I told you," Grayson said with a grin, thrusting the game into the air. "I'm not going to be able to sleep now."

"Wouldn't that just be the worst trick if you got a game, but not the system," Harvey said deviously.

Grayson's eyes sank to the floor. "You wouldn't really do that, would you? I've been asking for it for like three years."

Harvey shrugged his shoulders and said, "I think it's time for bed." It *was* an evil trick, but as an adult having lived through overly sarcastic parents, it was nice to see the tradition continue.

Grayson ran to his room, a bubble of excitement and dread hanging over him. We tucked the girls in, read stories and gave kisses, then walked back into the kitchen to finish wrapping gifts and open another bottle of wine.

"They have you working on Christmas Eve huh?" I asked, tearing off a piece of tape.

"Unfortunately. You wouldn't believe the amount of pressure I'm under." Harvey drank half of his glass of wine. "The company is looking to expand. The CEO said he needed me in the office tomorrow by three." Shaking his head, he drank the rest, setting his empty glass down on the table. I looked up in time to see that this was the first Angela was hearing about it, her face pinched and angry.

"Really?" I said, pushing a gift to the side. "On Christmas day."

Harvey nodded as he poured a second glass. "But you know what I told Craig." Harvey's head shot up. "I told him that the only way that was happening was if he came here, looked my wife and kids in the eyes, and told them himself."

Stunned, I dropped the tape that was in my hands. Angela slowly walked to Harvey's side, wrapping her arms around his waist. "I hope you still have a job after that," I said.

Harvey chuckled, swirling the wine in his glass. "As a matter-of-fact, I got a bonus." He turned and planted a kiss on Angela's cheek. "He said that in thirty years of being CEO, no one has ever stood up to him like that. He admired the size of my balls and handed me a check for forty thousand dollars."

"What!" Angela shouted, slapping him on the arm and stepping backwards. "You're joking."

"I can't make something like that up. He said that twenty years ago he promised himself that the first person to put him in his place and show him he was too focused on his work and not the wellbeing of his employees, he would write them a check for forty grand."

"That stuff only happens in movies," I said, clapping him on the shoulder. "So you weren't working then?"

"No, I was looking at the bank account to make sure I wasn't dreaming." He walked to the living and returned with his computer. "See," he said, pointing at the screen. "He also said not to come back until after the new year."

Angela threw her arms around his neck as tears trickled down her face, landing safely on his shoulder.

Placing the last of the gifts under the tree, I congratulated Harvey again, shaking his hand. After hugging Angela, I walked to the guest room, head swirling from wine, and fell asleep. My body shook like an earthquake in the morning. The girls all piled onto the bed, giggling and jumping up and down.

"Get up," Grayson said, standing by the door. "Get up, get up," the girls echoed.

I rolled to my side and slid my aching legs off the bed, stretching my arms over my head with a yawn. "It's time already?" I asked, a hint of playful annoyance in my voice.

Vivian reached over and pinched my cheeks, shouting, "Yes, yes, yes."

"Alright, I guess I'll come downstairs."

A row of mugs sat on the kitchen island filled with warm apple cider. Taking mine, I stood in front of the deck window watching as the white caps disappeared in the sand. I'll never get used to not seeing snow on the ground for Christmas but having the ocean as a replacement isn't the worst thing in the world.

"Have a seat everyone," Angela said as she walked into the living room.

They opened each gift with pure intensity, a confetti of wrapping paper bursting through the air. Kristi and Margo sat on the floor across from each other, their feet connected in a diamond, their presents piled between them. Paula sat in one of the bar stools in the kitchen, her hands moving from gift to gift, unsure which to play with first. Vivian brought her gifts to the back deck, away from everyone, saying, 'she wanted to be uninterrupted, so she could color coordinate.' Grayson piled most of his gifts to the side. In front of him was an Xbox and a thirty-two-inch flat screen television. "Will you help me set it up," he asked, looking up at his father. Nodding his head, Harvey sprung from his seat, lifted the tv off the ground and headed up the steps.

"I remember when a new shirt and five dollars to spend on candy at the movies was enough to get me excited," I said, placing my arm around Angela.

"It's a different world." She rested her head on my shoulder.

"You're telling me. We're seven years post terrorist attack, the Red Sox won the World Series again and we have a black president." I took a deep breath and looked down at the twins as they held hands and rocked back and forth.

"And Harvey's *home* for Christmas." She lifted her head and walked to the back deck, sliding the door open and poking her head out. "Why don't you finish up and help me get lunch ready?" Vivian nodded her head and placed a pair of blue socks next to her blue hair ties.

"Will you run up and tell the boys lunch will be ready in about twenty minutes?" she asked, starting the stove top and walking to the refrigerator.

I walked up the spiral, rugged staircase and into Grayson's room. Harvey was leaning over Grayson's dresser with wires in his hand.

"Angela said lunch in twenty," I said, taking a seat next to Grayson on his bed. "You sure he knows what he's doing?"

Grayson nudged my side and laughed. "I trust him more than you.".

"Now just turn this on and... bang." Harvey stepping back and admiring his work. "You're all set." He clapped his hands together and sat on the other side.

"Thanks dad," Grayson pressed a button on his controller and the screen flashed several images.

"I know your mother said this stuff would rot your brain. But, hey, why not rot your brain doing something fun." He ruffled Grayson hair and kissed him on the top of the head. "One game and then downstairs for lunch okay?" Grayson shook his head, his eyes glued to the screen.

Aside from seeing family, the food was the best part about being in Florida for Christmas. Taking our seats around the table, Angela placed a giant bowl of fish chowder in the middle. We each had our own miniature loaf of freshly baked bread and a bowl for fruit salad. Not the most traditional Christmas meal but well worth it.

"I can't tell if you liked it," Angela said, turning her head on its side.

Smiling, I licked the empty bowl and sent it spinning on the table. Vivian pounded her fist on the table and cheered.

"I haven't even taken my seat yet and you've finished a bowl." Angel shook her head and waddled to the table with a glass of iced tea. "I guess it's a good thing I made extra."

"You are a mother, and Italian," Harvey said.

She shot him a playful glare and spooned herself a ladle of chowder. "When are you leaving, Uncle Sal?" Vivian asked through a mouthful.

"Do you want me gone so soon?" I let my mouth drop and my eyes droop with sadness.

"No, of course not!"

"Okay, good. I will be here for two and a half more months. But I will be working most of the time. I have to finish the story I'm writing before I go back to New York."

"What if I don't want you to go back?" Her eyes began to well, her spoon slipping from her fingers and onto the table.

I wrapped my arm around her shoulder and said, "Don't worry, I'm only a phone call away, and maybe one of these days, your parents will bring you up to the city to visit me and your uncle Mike."

"Fat Uncle Mike. He's funny," Vivian said, snatching up her spoon.

What had been in Angela's mouth was now scattered across the table. "I'm so sorry honey," she said, wiping Harvey's arm with a napkin. "I was not expecting that."

"It's what Grayson always calls him," she said with a shrug of her shoulders. With a grin, I said, "I'm not complaining, because that means I'm not the fat one."

Harvey laughed, raising his glass in the air. Angela looked sideways at Grayson who was trying to hide behind his bread and the twins attempted to make a song of it all. Soon the room was loud and boisterous, exactly what an Italian meal should be.

As we cleared the table, Grayson snuck back to his room to play while all the girls piled into the living room to watch *A Christmas Story*. I found myself eager to hear the crashing waves. As I sat on the back porch, I thought of Mary-Ann and wondered if this would be the last Christmas she'd ever remember. I hoped it wouldn't, but if it were, I also hoped it was the greatest Christmas she'd ever have.

Chapter 7

March 2009

There are two types of people in the world. City folk, and everyone else. And after the four months I spent by the beach, I was happy to be home. There's nothing like a whiff of hotdogs and pretzels followed by a burst sewage line and fresh tar. The sound of honking cabs, yelling, and street performers. But, there's a quietness about it. If you don't listen too closely, all the sounds come together, and it is almost symphonic. Early in my career, I'd often find myself on street benches with my pad allowing the city to help guide my pen.

In a city like New York, it becomes smaller and smaller the longer you live there. Each block runs into the next. The same constructions being done at every corner. A newsstand sits across the street near a deli, pawnshop, pizzeria and barber. But I love it. The noise lets me know that I'm still alive and the people account for endless entertainment.

I sat at the edge of my bed rubbing the night from my eyes. Scout was flipped on his back snoring, his legs twitching as if he were chasing a rabbit. My buzzer went off and I stood up and walked to the door.

"Who is it?" I said through the intercom.

"Ryan. Can you let me up?"

I buzzed him in and went to my bedroom to get dressed. "What is it?" I asked, starting my coffee machine.

"There's been a shooting."

I looked at him sideways. "There are shootings almost every day. Not that I take them lightly, but why is it so important that I'm aware?" I poured a cup, dropped in two cubes of sugar, and stirred.

"It was down by that soup kitchen you're always talking about."

"What! Why didn't anyone call me?" I set the cup down and rushed to my closet to grab a hat and pair of shoes.

"Allan said he tried but you didn't answer. I tried when I finished talking with him, but your phone went straight to voicemail."

I ran to my bedside table. My phone was fully charged but I forgot to turn it on when I got home from my trip. Scout jolted awake, looking around in a daze. "Damnit!" I said, rushing to the door.

"I've got my car parked outside, I'll take you over there," Ryan said, following close behind.

"Thanks. Was anyone there?" I asked as the elevator door closed.

"Allan said that, the ladies were there working, but he didn't think anyone inside was hurt."

"Okay. Just get onto fifth avenue and take that all the way to Forest Park. I'll tell you where to go from there," I said as we climbed into the car. The street was flooded with police. Yellow tape marked off half the block and the entrance to the building. I could see a few of the women speaking with officers, another leaning against the wall with her hands covering her face. Dozens of people stood at the edge of the tape frantically using their cameras to document the scene.

A police officer walked up shouting, "Please, everyone step…back." His arms waved through the air. The wail that came from the sidewalk was the most piercing noise I had ever heard. It took several men to pull the woman off the ground. She fought and clawed her way back, the scream growing louder and more violent. Two more officers approached, grabbed her by the arms and pulling her flailing body onto the street. Tears mixed with blood and smeared across her face. Katrina lay sobbing on the ground, her clothing covered in dirt. I approached slowly, my hands trembling as I sat beside her, cradling her head in my lap.

Ryan walked forward, pulling his badge from his pocket and showing it to the police. "Officer. My name is Ryan, from the Star Tribune. Can you tell me what's happened here?" he said, taking out his recorder.

"All we know at this point, is that there were several shots fired from what we believe was a moving vehicle." The officer turned and mumbled a few words into a walkie.

"Were they intended for the young man?"

"We cannot confirm at this time. Like I said, all we know is that there were several shots fired from what we believe was a moving vehicle." The officer shewed Ryan away and walked over to help cover the body with a tarp.

"We need everyone to please move back!" another officer yelled. "We cannot do our jobs safely if we have to worry about you as well. Please, move back." They extended the yellow tape even further, marking where shell casings and bullet holes were scattered across the ground.

I looked down at Katrina, her bronze skin glistening with sweat. Her screams had wilted, but her body convulsed in shock. Her arms and shirt were covered in blood. "Deep breaths. Take deep breaths," I said, stroking her brow.

"Ryan. Do you see that woman over there against the wall?" I said, pointing. "Yeah."

"Her name is Maxine. She volunteers here. Go ask her if she knows what happened."

As Ryan left, an EMT approached carrying a towel. "Hi, my name is Gabby. Can you help me get her on her feet and over to the ambulance?" I nodded my head.

"I need you to try and stand okay?" I said to Katrina, whose eyes rolled back and forth.

Throwing her arm around my shoulder, I carried most of her weight to the edge of the ambulance and set her down.

"I can take it from here. Thank you," Gabby said, ripping open a bag.

As I moved away, I felt a firm grip on my wrist. I looked back. Fear clung to her face. "Don't leave, please," Katrina whimpered.

"It's fine if she wants you to stay," Gabby said, handing me a sterilization wipe. "Use this to help me wipe the blood from her arms."

I held her hand in mine.

"She your wife?" Gabby asked, climbing into the ambulance. "No, just a friend."

"Okay. Well, she's still in a bit of shock and I need her to remove her shirt so I can bag it.

Do you think you can help me with that?" Gabby paused on the lip of the ambulance. "Sir!" I jerked my head. "Yes. Yes, of course. Just tell me what to do."

"I need you to hold her arms above her head so I can lift the shirt. If she begins to struggle, I may need to cut it off of her." Gabby slid a pair of scissors into her breast pocket and hopped back down to the ground. I took Katrina's arms as Gabby worked her shirt up and over her head. "Good. Now put this on her."

After helping her into a clean shirt her head fell heavily on my shoulder.

Ryan returned with Maxine.

"Oh Kat," she said, finding a seat on the other side and wrapping her arms around Katrina. "I'm so sorry."

"Ryan what did she say?" I asked.

"They didn't see anything. They were in the kitchen working when they heard the shots. I guess Katrina's son Malcolm was stopping by to get money for the movies. She was the first one to the door and when she looked out, he was lying face down on the ground." He looked over at her and shook his head.

"Did they see a car leaving?"

"Not that they can remember. Katrina screamed and ran to her son while Maxine called 911." Ryan pulled out his phone to show me an email he'd received from the office.

Remember Me

"You can go. I'll be fine here. Tell Calvin to take over the Brockswood piece on school lunches I was going to do for this weekend. And tell Amy what's happened. I'll gather as much information as I can, but I'll need your help writing this piece."

"Alright. Call me tonight. I don't want you going home without talking to someone." Ryan and I shook hands and I watched him leave, his pale skin bobbing in and out of the dark background.

I rode in the ambulance with Katrina, my hand gripping hers as she lay on the stretcher.

Her body had calmed but her mind was still elsewhere, the images of her son floating by in between blinks, each bump in the road like a gunshot passing through his innocent body.

Aaron and Allan met us at the hospital. They sat with me in the waiting area while Maxine went into the room. SpongeBob played quietly overhead as two young children bounced up and down, eyes glued to the television.

"What happened?" Allan asked.

"I didn't get much more out of the police before we left. Apparently, he was coming to get money for the movies from Katrina when they heard gunfire. The police believe it was a drive-by shooting, but they haven't confirmed yet."

"Damn shame," Allan spat.

"Yeah," I said, pulling my leg up onto my thigh. "Where's Mary-Ann?" I asked. "She's at home with Prince. He's back in town for a few weeks," Allan said.

"How is she feeling? I was going to stop in this afternoon, but then all this happened."

Allan exhaled slowly. "Much worse. She goes days without remembering where she is or who I am. And she's not eating much." He ran his hand over his head.

Turning in my seat to face him, I said, "Have you considered what I said about finding someone to help. Someone professional?"

"More now than before. If she doesn't start eating, I'll have to admit her to the hospital." "It just doesn't make any sense," Aaron interrupted, rubbing his hands together. "That was the nicest kid I've ever met. There's no way he was involved with people who would do something that like."

There were several things that ran through my head, and that was one of them. Children are exposed to more in today's world than even thought possible when I was growing up. And children are the best at keeping the mask on when adults are around. But I knew Malcolm. He was a straight A student, captain of the chess club at Luther High, and voted president of the freshman class. He also performed at a high level on the basketball team and volunteered at Full Bellies every Saturday morning. Aaron was right. It just didn't make any sense.

"Maybe he was mistaken for someone else," Allan said. "That happens with gangs all the time. It's one of the reasons we bought a house out here."

"A random killing then?" Aaron suggested. "It's something gangs do to initiate new members."

I stood. "Speculation only leads to further disappointment. We should leave it to the police to figure out."

I poked my head in the doorway. Maxine rested her head on Katrina's hip. Katrina's eyes were closed and the rise and fall of her chest seemed calm.

I quietly closed the door. "It's three-thirty. I'm going to head into the office for an hour or so before going home for the night. I'll stop in tomorrow morning to see how she's doing."

"Thank you, Sal," Allan said.

I walked out feeling like my head was dragging against the floor. A weight not so unfamiliar tugging heavily on my heart.

"You didn't need to come in today, Sal," Ryan said as I sat down at my desk. "We've got things covered. Calvin is at Lakeview Elementary speaking with Principal Brockswood. Amy knows as much as we do and she hired a temp the other week to help with filing."

"I know, Ryan. But I couldn't just go home and sit there, I couldn't stay at the hospital, and I couldn't go back to the soup kitchen and see it all over again." I pulled open one of my drawers and removed a bottle of bourbon. Taking a drink, I smacked my lips together and returned the bottle. "You can have some if you want."

"No thanks, I had a drink of my own at the bar across the street before coming in. I haven't been out in the field since college, and I sure as hell wasn't gathering information on drive-by shootings." Ryan shook his head, closed the door, and sat.

"I've had a few in my thirty years, but never someone I knew." I reached for my drawer again, but thought better of it, taking my pen instead and rolling it across my knuckles.

A knock came at the door. Amy stood by the window with her hand to the side of her head like a phone and walked away.

"Hello?" I said, bringing my phone to my ear.

"Hi, Mr. Pitello. This is Alise, Sharice's daughter."

"Yes, Alise. How are you?"

"I think I should be asking you that question," she said, her voice filled with sympathy. "I just got off the phone with Maxine. She said the police came to the hospital to speak with Katrina."

I quickly put the phone back down and slid a pad and pen to Ryan. "I've got you on speaker. I'm in my office with my editor Ryan. How is Katrina doing? When I left, she was asleep. What did Maxine say?"

Alise cleared her throat. "They had to wake her, but Maxine said Katrina was able to talk. She said they asked her if her son was involved in any gang activity."

"Was he?" I asked, jotting down the word gang and circling it.

"She said no, of course not. He would never do something like that."

"What else? Did they confirm whether the shots were fired from a vehicle?" I asked. "They said they found tire marks that would indicate a car left in a hurry, but there weren't any witnesses to determine what type of car it was, so it will take longer to confirm. Sal," she said, her voice lowering to a whisper.

"Yes. What is it?"

"Katrina was pretty upset that you weren't there when she woke up. I know you two haven't spent much time together, but I think she finds comfort in having you around."

"If you hear from Maxine again, tell her to let Katrina know I'll come by in the morning. I still have a job to do, but I will be there with her as much as I can."

"Thank you, Sal. That means a lot. I'm going to Full Bellies to see if I can get some answers."

Gabriel Fowler

"Alright, thanks for calling Alise. Let me know if you hear anything else. I'll be in touch."

After hanging up, I wrote down a few more things, peeled the sticky note and stuck it to the calendar on my desk.

"Call the police station every two hours until you leave tonight," I said as I stood. "Okay. Where are you going?" Ryan asked.

"Home. This was not what I expected to fall into the day after getting back from my trip. I need another strong drink and some rest. I'll call you in the morning." Ryan nodded his head and walked back to his desk.

Four days later, I sat in the front pew of the Big House, Katrina's tears soaking to the bone of my shoulder as she wept, the casket just feet away. No parent should ever have to bury their child. The thought alone is hard enough to comprehend.

After speaking with the police and a witness that eventually came forward, we learned that two suspects were brought into custody. It was a random shooting. Another fourteen-year-old kid who thought that joining a gang would give him everything he ever wanted. Instead, it tore a mother to pieces, shattered the safety of a community and would find him in prison for over a decade.

The church began to fill with people. They dressed in the mourning black and carried white flowers, placing them gently on the casket as they walked by. The choir sang in mumbled tones, their robes swaying gently from left to right.

Aaron sat behind me, grabbing my shoulder and greeting me with a furrowed brow. I turned and saw Allan slowly pushing Mary-Ann in a wheelchair. It was the first time I'd seen her since leaving for Florida. She looked brittle then, but now she looked of skin and bone. She wore a flowery hat and her eyes wandered about the room. Allan took his seat at the end of the pew and rolled her up beside him, just as Bishop Anderson began to speak. I had no pen and pad, no computer, no recorder. I was there, a comfort for a hurting friend. Though I'm usually far better at remembering what is happening around me, I cannot recall anything that was said, or what preceded thereafter. Just the blurred vision of white flowers, the warm tears upon my shoulder and the scream that still haunts me to this day.

It would be months before Katrina would see anyone, including me, though I would stop by and knock gently on her door. Overwhelmed, I knew I needed to put my energy back into Mary-Ann, the reason I became part of this community in the first place.

Chapter 8

June 2009

"Dad, she needs help. You need help," Prince said, sitting on the front porch.

Prince had called me the night before to ask if I would come by. He wanted help convincing Allan that Mary-Ann should be somewhere that could provide her with the care she needs.

"She's my wife," Allan spat, tears pouring down his face.

"And she's our mother." Prince walked to his side and wrapped his arms around his father. "You have to understand that this isn't just about her. You are going to kill yourself having looked after her every day. Dad, it's not healthy."

Aaron stood in the doorway with a cup of coffee in his hand. "He's right pops. Your body won't be able to handle it much longer."

Mary-Ann was asleep in the living room, her body cocooned in a blanket. Allan took several breaths. "It's just so hard for me to let her go."

"Allan," I said, standing. "You're not letting her go at all. There's nothing stopping you from being right there by her side the whole way through. This will just relieve some of the pressure." He nodded his head, but I could tell he was still reluctant to agree. "Think of it this way. There are likely things that are happening to her, both physically and mentally that you aren't even aware of that could lead to considerable damage. But if you take her somewhere, they will be able to better monitor her progress."

"Progress!" Allan shouted. "What progress?"

"Dad, he's just trying to help," Aaron said, stepping onto the porch.

"I honestly believe that there is room for progression. But if she stays here, the likelihood of that happening isn't very high." I moved forward and put my arm on his shoulder. "I want to see her back to the way she was more than you could possibly know. I never had the chance to see Mary-Ann before she got sick. You all did. Remember that. Remember how loving, joyful, forgiving, selfless, compassionate. The list goes on, Al."

Prince helped his father to a chair. Looking up at me, he mouthed the words, *thank you.*

"Alright," Allan said. "What do we do first?"

Aaron finished what was left of his coffee and set the mug down on the railing. "I think we should take her to a doctor to get her assessed first. We can't know the help she needs if we don't know what all the issues are."

"I agree," Prince said, sitting in the chair next to his father. "But we don't want you to think we are taking sides. We want you to be a part of the decision."

Allan looked at them both and nodded. "You're right. Call the doctor's office and make an appointment. The sooner the better, and we'll go from there." He turned his focus to me. "I don't think I ever thanked you for what you did for Katrina. You didn't have to."

"I'm glad you called Allan. I would have done it for any of those women. Meeting you and your family has revealed an entirely new appreciation of life for me."

"Us black folk aren't too bad eh." He smiled, rubbing the dried tears from his eyes.

"Not at all Al. Not at all."

<>

"Doctor said she's twelve pounds underweight and losing a lot of nutrients," Prince said over the phone a few days later. "She's been admitted to the Rehabilitation Ward. He's unsure how long she'll need to be there based on what he saw, but she may need to be transferred to the psychiatric building."

"What do you mean?" I asked.

"The doctor ran several stress tests and he saw an increase in anxiety and locational discomfort. He said that could lead to sudden outbursts of aggression, which at her age would likely be more harmful to her than anyone else. Also, she would have a higher tendency to move about and go places in an attempt to find something she thought was familiar."

"I guess that's why she wandered off that day," I said. I was sitting in my office making corrections on another story.

"Exactly. But we didn't really give her an opportunity to wander off again because someone was always there watching her."

"Is she allowed visitors?" I asked, re-writing a sentence for the fifth time.

"We were told any time except the hours of one to three. They are doing intensive therapy to help her regain strength and cognitive function. She hasn't eaten much, so they're putting her on a diet as well. We told them a feeding tube should be a last resort."

"What about your father? How is he taking all of this?" I asked, finally happy with my sentence.

Prince chuckled. "Still stubborn. He wasn't happy that she would be spending this many nights away from the house, but we calmed him down enough to sign the paperwork. I swear man."

"Yeah, but you've got to understand where he's coming from."

"True. I'd see myself reacting the same way if my wife were in this position. Have you spoken with Katrina?" he asked.

"She took my call the other day, but only for about five minutes."

"She'll come around. You mean a lot to her, I know that. Maxine told me that she would go on and on about that *little Italian.*" He laughed, and I could hear a car door closing.

"As long as someone is checking on her, I'm happy."

"She's got plenty of support. Alright, well, I'm headed back home for a while. Miss the wife and the business needs me. Let me know if you need anything. I'll be back in about a month."

"Sounds good Prince. Be safe, I'll chat with you later." I hung up, the feeling of several weights sliding off my shoulders. Mary-Ann needed this. Allan needed it too even if he was too stubborn to believe it.

◇

Remember Me

I was blown away a few weeks later when I visited the Rehabilitation Ward. It was nothing like the rest of the hospital. The walls were covered in finger paintings, each room's floor tiled in an assortment of color. The hallway was etched in yellow painted bricks allowing for the magic of the Wizard of Oz. Nurses worked alongside patients ranging from four to one- hundred, all seeking to regain their health.

As I walked the yellow brick road, I stopped at a long desk covered in Polaroid pictures of smiling faces. A young man sat in a chair helping a little girl braid a beaded bracelet. I waited patiently for them to finish, her eyes lighting up as he tied it around her wrist.

"Thank you, Nurse Benson," she said as she ran off.

He turned and was surprised to see I was standing there. "Hello," he said, standing. "I hope you weren't waiting too long. I am Nurse—"

"Benson," I finished with a smile. "I didn't want to interrupt. That was really amazing what you did."

"I've had a lot of practice. I've been working here for about two years and I can honestly say I've made more of those than the average mom. I had to watch a video just to figure out how to do it." He laughed, showing a sparklingly white smile. "How can I help you?"

"My name is Sal Pitello. I was hoping I could see Mary-Ann Cauldwell."

"Are you on the visitors list?" he asked, reaching for a clipboard.

"I sure hope so," I said.

Nurse Benson ran his finger down the page. Shaking his head, he flipped to the next and repeated the process. "Ah, there it is. Sal Pitello. Says here you are a good friend to the family with no restrictions." He set the clipboard down and opened a drawer. "This is our visitor's lanyard. You must wear it at all times, and it must be returned at the end of your visit. Just go ahead and sign here next to your name for today's date, and I'll walk you to her room."

I signed quickly, tossing the pen into a colorful cup and walked by Nurse Benson's side. "I have to say, I wasn't expected to see all this life. The walls, the...yellow brick road. It's rather impressive."

"What is rehabilitation if we sit in dark rooms just talking about it? That's why this place has been so successful. We don't just talk about giving life back to our patients, we show them how it should be done. I was lucky to find a job here. I'm the only new hire in this department in the last twenty-three years." Nurse Benson took a left down a hallway. There were three rooms on each side and a window at the end that overlooked the west side of the city. "These people know what they're doing, and they love it."

"How *did* you then? Get a position here," I asked, admiring the artwork on the wall.

"To start, my mother works here. But one of their longtime head nurses became ill and chose to retire." He led me to the second room on the left.

Peeking through the door, I could see Mary-Ann sitting in a cushioned chair next to a partially opened window overlooking a small park. Her hair was combed out and hung in loose curls around her ears. She wore a green sweater, black pants, and a pair of slippers in the shape of a flower.

Nurse Benson knocked gently on the door. "Mary-Ann," he whispered. She turned her head and looked, her face still faded and discolored. "There's someone here to see you."

"How wonderful," she said, swiveling in her seat. She looked past Nurse Benson, made eye contact with me and smiled. "Mr. Pitello. It's great to see you. How is your story coming along?"

"You remember," I said, raising my hand to my chest, shocked to find that she recognized me. "Of course, I do. You're the one that's going to make me famous. I'd be a fool to forget you." She folded her hands on her lap. "Come sit with me. There are some children playing in the park."

"I'll leave you for now. If you need anything you know where to find me. In case of an emergency, press this button," Nurse Benson said, pointed to a large red button on the wall. "Someone will be by in an hour to take her to lunch."

"Thank you," I said, shaking his hand.

I fell gracefully into the seat beside Mary-Ann, throwing my arm over the armrest and looking out at the children playing in a pile of leaves. A small boy with a blue hat took a running start and launch himself into the air. The others laughed and threw leaves on top of him when he landed.

"To be that young again," Mary-Ann said, reaching over and taking hold of my hand. "I bet you'll be feeling that young in no time." I turned, her drooping brown eyes and freckled face staring back at me. "Have you been eating?" I ask, reaching over and placing my other hand on hers.

"Yes, the food is fabulous. They won't let me help in the kitchen though. I told them I've got over fifty years of experience preparing food," she giggled.

"There's no doubt in my mind you have the skill, but it's time that people took care of you for a change. They need to give you a little bell and a butler that will come running when you call."

"You stop that," Mary-Ann said, slapping me on the shoulder. With deep breath, Mary-Ann leaned forward, resting her arms on the windowsill.

"Tell me something Mama."

"What would you like to know Mr. Pitello?"

Remember Me

"Your fondest memory."

Mary-Ann thought for a long while, the wind whistling through the window. "Broadway," she said, laying her right cheek on her arms and closing her eyes. "Prince surprised us with tickets to Les Miserable. We had talked about going for years but never had the money."

The way her lips twitched and her eyes darted back and forth under their lids, I could tell she was there, standing in line to get in. A beautiful dress of violet with flowers in her hair. Allan in a black suit and plum tie standing next to her, arms linked and smiles rippling across their faces.

"He said that he was going to bring a date and he'd meet us at the theatre. So, Allan and I went out to dinner nearby and found our seats twenty minutes before the show. Ten minutes went by and there was no sign of Prince. Another five and the stage lights began to dim. I was starting to get worried when Allan began frantically shaking my arm. 'Look. Mary-Ann, look." He folded the program over and handed it to me, pointing at the cast list. I couldn't believe my eyes." Mary-Ann sat up, her mouth wide with a smile. "Jean Valjean played by Prince Cauldwell. And in parenthesis it said, 'we are happy to present the youngest, and first African American to star in this leading role."

Mary-Ann clapped her hands as tears trickled down her face. Her head began to sway as if listening to her son sing once again.

"Wow. I had no idea he performed on Broadway," I said, making a mental note to bring that up the next time I saw him.

"Yes, for several years actually. We thought he was working with his brother in Boston the summer after he graduated from college, but he was actually living just miles away, rehearsing for the show."

"How was he?" I asked.

"There's not a day that goes by that I don't think about that night. From the moment he walked on stage and started singing, till I laid my head down to sleep, I don't think I stopped crying. His voice was so powerful, so effortless, it was like God himself was singing." She wrapped her arms around herself and squeezed, inhaling deeply. "We found out his brothers and sisters were there too, in the upper balcony."

"Did they know before the show that Prince was in it?" I asked, standing and walking to a sink to get a glass of water.

"Oh, yes. Prince told them that if Allan or I asked what he was up too, to say that he was in Boston."

"So, it was all for you. I can understand why that is a memory that you're most fond of."

"There are others, but that stands out the most." I went back to my seat and stood behind it, my arms resting on the back. "Will you eat lunch with me?" Mary-Ann asked.

"I'd love to. Afterwards, if it's allowed, I can take you down to the park. Get some fresh air." I walked to the corner of the room and rolled her wheelchair over.

"That would be lovely," she said, holding out her hand. I helped her into the wheelchair and met her nurse in the hallway.

"Mrs. Cauldwell. I was just coming by to get you." Her red hair bounced in long curls and a fade of freckles hid behind a pair of green glasses. "You must be Mr. Pitello," she said, holding out her hand.

"Call me Sal," I said.

"I'm Nurse Proctor and I've had the pleasure of getting to know Mary-Ann quite well over the past few weeks." She took over the pushing of the wheelchair down the hallway, to the left and into a large cafeteria filled with people. "She likes her sweets." Nurse Proctor leaned down and whispered something, causing Mary-Ann to burst with laughter. "It sounds like it's been a good day."

"Better now that you're here," Mary-Ann said. She looked up at me and all recognition seemed to vanish. "Why is this man following us?" she asked, turning back to nurse Proctor.

"Sweetheart, this is Sal Pitello. The man writing the story. He'd like to eat lunch with you, if that's alright."

"And go down to the park to get some fresh air," I said, squatting down. "Oh yes, right. Sal. It's so nice to see you."

Nurse Proctor set Mary-Ann's chair next to a table and we walked together to get the food. "Even the simplest of changes can alter her train of thought and confuse her," she said, grabbing a plate and a set of plastic utensils. I took the same for myself. "Our little trade off with the wheelchair was enough for her to forget me?"

"Sometimes. It all depends on the day and certain stimuli. I've had patients that cry out for a loved one that is literally sitting right next to them. It's by far one of the worst diseases I've ever dealt with." After loading a sandwich, a few pieces of fruit and stack of chocolate chip cookies onto the plate, we walked back to the table.

"Mr. Pitello, thank you for having lunch with me," Mary-Ann said. "My pleasure."

"Alright Mary-Ann, I'm going to confidently leave you in the hands of Sal. He'll take you down to the park after you've finished eating and I'll see you before you head in for therapy.

Does that sound like a plan?" Nurse Proctor said. Mary-Ann shook her head and smiled.

Remember Me

Lunch was quiet. Mary-Ann focused on her food more than anything else and I was happy to sit back and watch. Her head tip-toed back and forth to a silent tune as she bit into her cookies. Although her body seemed weak, her spirits were high. I wondered if Allan had seen her like this, 'normal.' I had hoped that he could take care of himself with the time away, maybe even enjoyed it a little bit. But, if I knew him, he'd likely be more anxious now than he was when Mary-Ann was home. We finished lunch and I pushed Mary-Ann to a nearby elevator. A mother carrying an infant stepped out as we were getting on and Mary-Ann commented on how cute the little girl's outfit was.

The July, New York heat sprinted at us as we walked outside. The air was moist and thick, but Mary-Ann raised her arms in the air and took a deep, joyful breath. "Did I ever tell you about Prince being on Broadway?" she asked as I pushed her to the park bench. The children were now sitting in the grass next to a woman listening to her read a story.

"I can't say you did," I said, happy to hear the story and see her face light up again. I sat, my arm draped over the back of the bench. As she began, I closed my eyes, picturing a young, handsome Prince Cauldwell singing Jean Valjean's, Who Am I.

Gabriel Fowler

Who am I?
Can I condemn this man to slavery?
Pretend I do not feel his agony,
This innocent who bears my face,
Who goes to judgement in my place,
Who am I?

Mary-Ann finished with tears in her eyes and her hands clasped together under her chin. One of the children, the small boy with the hat, suddenly walked up. He stood on the sidewalk with his head tilted to the side.

"Are you sad?" he asked. "I can hug you if you're sad. My mom always hugs me when I'm sad or scared and it makes me feel better." Before I could do anything, he lunged forward, collapsing in Mary-Ann's lap and wrapping his arms around her neck.

Mary-Ann chuckled, patting him gently on the back. "I'm not sad little one. But thank you for the hug."

"Landon!" the woman shouted. "Come back over here and leave them alone." The boy stood up, shrugged his shoulders and skipped back over to the grass. Laughing, I said, "Well that was a surprise."

"It sure was. Makes me think of my grandchildren and how long it's been since they bounced on my lap." Mary-Ann stared off at the group of children, her lips thinning to a smile. My phone buzzed. Ryan sent me a text about the edits he'd been working on. I responded quickly before putting my phone back in my pocket.

"It's almost time for your therapy and I need to stop at the office before I check on Kristina," I said, unlocking the wheels and pushing her back towards the building. "Will you come see me again?" she asked.

"Of course, I will. Hopefully at the end of the week."

"Allan should be by tonight. He said he likes to see me off into the night."

Nurse Proctor was waiting for us in the lobby when we arrived. "Ready for therapy?" she asked, kneeling and placing a hand on Mary-Ann's arm. "Ready now that you're here," she laughed, grabbing nurse Proctor's hand and shaking it.

"It was nice meeting you," I said with a wave. Nurse Proctor smiled, her dimples sinking deep within her cheeks. I waved to Nurse Benson as well before pushing the door open and heading back outside.

Chapter 9

Aaron was standing outside of the room when I came to see her again. His face bore two, long scratches and he dabbed his cheek with a tissue. A scream came from the room, followed by the clang of metal.

"What is going on?" I said.

"She's losing it. She hasn't gone to therapy, eaten or taken her medication in three days. She's having fits of rage and keeps saying we are strange men trying to torture her." He looked down at the tissue, then back up at me.

"And I'm guessing she did that?" I said with a nod.

"Yeah," he said. "I tried to give her a hug and she swiped her hand at me." He tried to smile but it came off more painful and forced. "I don't know what to do."

"It's so strange," I said, looking in through the window of the room. Allan was standing on one side of the bed next to Nurse Proctor. Mary-Ann stood on the other, a bedpan in one hand and her other holding the back of a chair for support. "I was here Monday. She recognized me the moment I walked in. We spoke for an hour before having lunch together and then went out to the park. Just days later she's a completely different person?"

"Stop coming here!" Mary-Ann shouted, swinging the bedpan and almost losing her balance. "I told you already, I have nothing you want. Why won't you just leave me alone?"

"It's impossible to explain," Aaron said. He stepped to the door and slowly pushed it open.

"Go!" Mary-Ann screeched. Allan tried to move around the bed to close the gap between them and was struck with the bedpan. He stumbled backwards. Aaron stepped forward and caught him.

"Calm down Mary-Ann, we just want to help." Nurse Proctor raised her hands in front of her body. "Please, tell us how we can help?"

"You can all leave me alone." Mary-Ann was losing her breath, her body sinking further into the chair. She fell, missing the seat and crashed to the ground. Nurse Proctor rushed forward.

"We need to get her on the bed and sedated. We can't afford another outburst like that. It could send her body into shock and cause another stroke." Aaron and I lifted Mary-Ann off the floor and set her gently on the bed. Nurse Proctor inserted the IV and placed an oxygen mask over her face. Nurse

Proctor took a deep breath, her hands gripping her hips. "I wasn't expecting that," she said. "She's certainly still got her strength."

"I just wish she wasn't using it against us," Aaron said, helping his father into a chair. "Is she going to be alright," Allan asked as he wiped his face with a kerchief. "The whole reason for bringing her here was for her to get better. What are you doing to make her—" Aaron cut him off before he raised his voice.

"I assure you Mr. Cauldwell. I, as well as the rest of the staff here are doing everything we can to help your wife recover, or at the very least, maintain." She was calm, poised and professional. "This is the best place for her, but you have to understand that there are going to be days, weeks, even months where the small battles are lost. But if we work together, we can hopefully win the war."

Mary-Ann groaned softly, then fell into a deep sleep. "When she wakes, we try again," Nurse Proctor said, walking to the door. "In the meantime, go get something to eat." She closed the door behind her, and the room fell to a dull silence.

"If I don't see any progress in the next couple weeks, I'm taking her home with me," Allan said after a long while. Aaron stood and walked to the window. It was raining, and the wind blew, making it appear as if the trees were dancing, their branches weaving in an intricate pattern.

"Don't be ridiculous, Dad," Aaron groaned.

"I'm not being ridiculous. If it goes on like this, I'll be paying them to do the same thing I was doing."

"She's eaten more here in the last week than she did the last two months she was at home. I'm sorry, but I won't allow it. Prince and I are also on the paperwork and it must to be a majority decision."

"You're going to team up against me to keep her here even if she's not getting any better," Allan said, his words getting caught in his throat.

"Dad stop thinking we are trying to make things harder for you. You need help taking care of her, and she needs help being taken care off. It's that simple." Aaron walked back to where Allan was sitting. "This is what's best for her, at least for now. I promise you, I will carry her out of this place myself the second I don't see it benefitting her."

Allan rubbed his eyes with his palms. "Alright."

"Alright," Aaron said, exhaling heavily. "Should we go get something to eat then?" he asked, extending an arm to help Allan to his feet.

Allan grabbed Aaron's hand and said, "I hope they have ice cream."

Aaron laughed as he turned toward the door. "Shit. Sal, I completely forgot you were here."

"I didn't feel it was appropriate to interrupt," I said, holding the door open. "I'll join you for a meal if you don't mind."

The cafeteria was bustling when we walked in. *Happy* by Pharrell played in the background and colorful signs reading, *Fat Friday* and *Fun Friday,* were displayed all over the room. A group of ladies and young children stood by the entrance handing out bead necklaces and crafts they had made throughout the week.

"It's a doggy," a little girl said, thrusting a paper plate that was painted to look like a pug into my hands.

"It looks amazing," I said. She smiled and wrapped her little arms around my leg. "Mom will love this when she's able to come down here," Aaron said as we took our seats. Allan grunted, sticking his fork into a pile of mashed potatoes.

"She told me she wanted to help in the kitchen," I said, trying to break the silence. Aaron laughed. "Sounds like her. I'm not sure if I had a meal in my first twenty-five years that she didn't have her hands in." He took a bite of his sandwich and wipe his face. "So, how's Katrina doing?"

"She saw me for the first time yesterday," I said, toying with my food. "It looked like she hadn't eaten or showered in a while. She let me bring her to the couch in her living room and I made her a cup of tea." Aaron nodded his head, his face filled with compassion.

"She didn't speak much. Just grunted to my yes or no questions and when I tried to put my arm around her, she flinched and started crying." Quickly losing my appetite, I pushed the food away and sat back in my chair, my emotions a clear contrast to the boisterous room. "It's interesting. I've spent my entire adult life so plugged into my job that I've never really known what it felt like to care for someone like I do Katrina. And I've only known her for such a short time."

"She has that effect of people," Allan said, unwrapping his brownie. "She's kind, positive, always looking to put others before herself."

"She has a good heart. I can't necessarily say I care for her in a romantic way yet, but terrible things like that shouldn't happen to good people."

Allan took a sip of water to clear his throat and said, "That is the age-old question and one I've been struggling with myself. Where do you think Katrina learned how to love people?" he said, winking. "It's part of the reason I fell in love with Mary-Ann, and why it's so difficult to see her in a place like this."

"I heard that they are thinking of putting Malcolm on the wall," Aaron said.

I nodded my head. "Yeah, I spoke with Alise the other day and the son of the man who painted the mural said he would do it for free."

"Katrina will really appreciate that," Allan said, taking another bite of his brownie.

A boy of thirteen wearing a Miami Heat jersey stopped at the table with a pitcher of water. "Would any of you like your cups refilled?" he asked. His left leg was in a brace that went from his thigh to his ankle.

"Certainly, young man," Allan said, passing his cup to the end of the table. "What's your name?"

"Ethan," he said, pouring the water and handing the cup back.

"What are you in for?" Allan said, snickering. The boy turned his head in confusion. "Your leg. What happened?"

"Oh, right," Ethan said, setting the pitcher down. "Well, I was playing baseball and crushed one out to right field. I took off down the first base line and I could hear my team yelling and cheering." His voice became heavy and full. "The first base coach waved me to second. I could feel my helmet bouncing up and down and it almost fell off my head."

Aaron looked at me with a huge smile.

"I looked out halfway to second and saw that the right fielder was about to throw. I charged forward and slid, smashing into second base just before he caught the ball. It all happened so fast. My leg got caught under the base, but my body kept moving forward and bang!" he shouted, exploding his hands away from each other. "My leg shattered in like a million pieces." By the end, Ethan was out of breath.

"You're quite the storyteller," I said, tapping my hand on the table. Both Allan and Aaron nodded in agreement.

"Thanks. It didn't even hurt either," he said proudly, grabbing the pitcher. "How long do you have to be in that thing?" Aaron asked, pointing at his leg.

"Another six months. I had to learn how to walk again, and they said I have to keep wearing this for stability. It itches like crazy though." Ethan shrugged his shoulders, reminding me of how unstoppable teenage boys think they are.

"I bet it does. Well, good luck," I said. Ethan nodded and hobbled away.

"If that doesn't put a smile on your face, I don't know what will," Aaron said, grabbing our plates and stacking them at the end of the table. "

"Nice boy," Allan said. "He'll be back on the field before he knows it with that attitude."

"Mr. Cauldwell," a voice said behind me. I turned to find nurse Proctor standing with her hands on her hips. "Not to alarm you, but your wife is awake. She is unclear of where she is, but she's non-aggressive. Would you like to come back and try speaking with her?"

"Yes, of course," Allan said as he stood.

"I'll take care of the clean-up. The two of you should go," I said, pointing toward the door."

As I was collecting the trash, a boy and his father came by with wet clothes to wipe the table. I thanked them, threw our plates away and headed back down the hallway to Mary-Ann's room.

Allan sat in the chair next to the bed holding her left hand. Mary-Ann cupped Allan's face with her right and I could hear her whispering. Tears ran down Allan's face. Aaron stood at the foot of the bed, his brown coat hanging over his shoulder, gently squeezing her leg. Nurse Proctor walked from the room and stood next to me.

"What is she saying?" I asked.

"She just keeps repeating his name." Nurse Proctor wiped her eyes with a tissue. "It doesn't matter how many times you see it. It doesn't make it any easier to watch." She turned and walked away. I sat in a chair in the hallway taking pictures and jotting down notes for an hour. The music from the lunchroom was only a muffled thump, but parents with their children, elderly with their nurses and doctors continued to dance up and down the hallway. Aaron came to sit with me.

"She's seems pretty calm. I think my dad is going to stay with her a little while longer."

"Yeah. He must be relieved she recognized him." I said. I closed my notebook and stuffed it back into my bag.

"It's all he really cares about. He'd let her stay here forever if she knew who he was every time he walked through the door. I'm going to take the train back to the house and then head home. I'm sure my wife misses me."

I shook his hand and said goodbye, watching his shoulders begin to shrink as he walked, looking more and more like his father.

◇

The following week, Prince returned with his sons, Isaiah and Joseph, and offered to take me deep sea fishing. Isaiah was in his early thirties, six feet, stocky and knew more about fishing than I think I know about journalism. His brother, a few years younger, was there only to make us all laugh.

"Stop it, you moron," Isaiah said, throwing a chunk of fish at his brother. "What?" Joseph said as he dodged.

"You're such a dork man. That's not even how you're supposed to put the bait on the hook." Isaiah walked across the boat and stood next to his brother. "Let me see it."

"Nah bruv. Me got dis man. Don't worry. Me'a catch de fish b'for you," Joseph said, using a terrible, yet hilarious Jamaican accent.

"The fish are going to swim by and laugh," Isaiah said, shaking his head and walking back to the other side.

Prince laughed and said, "Grown men and still having the same dumb arguments they were having as kids. The only difference is there aren't fists being thrown."

"Fist fights?" I asked, tying the hook onto my line.

"Oh yeah, they were at each other's throats for most of their life. Three years apart and interested in a lot of the same things. Competition was their middle name." Prince stuck his hand into a bucket and pulled out his bait. "I've seen them grow a lot closer over the past few years though."

"Were you like that with any of your brothers?" I asked.

"Of course. Paul and Luke were nearly done with high school when I was born so I didn't spend much time with him. But Aaron and I were five years apart and fought over the same things, especially when I grew taller than him. He felt he had to prove even more how much better he was at everything."

Remember Me

We walked to the front of the boat and threw our lines out. "And now?" I asked, slowing reeling in.

"Very much the same as Isaiah and Joseph. We still bicker and argue, but we tend to acknowledge and respect each other's strengths."

"Such a common theme with brothers. Mike and I were the same way. Three years apart, but we competed more over success in school. We weren't very athletic. It actually took us much longer to find common ground." My line was all the way back to the boat, so I threw it out again.

"What changed?" Prince asked.

"My father got sick. Mike and I were civil before then, but we realized how much of our lives we missed because we were too stubborn. When my father died, it really changed us. We hardly go a day without talking."

Prince set his pole in the rod holder and leaned against the railing. "You never mention your father passing away," he said.

"I told you, sucka!" Joseph shouted. We looked over and saw him struggling to reel. Out in the water a massive sailfish broke the surface, its tail whipping through the air. Excited, we rushed to his side.

"Be careful," Isaiah said.

"Don't worry, I got this." Joseph began pulling hard on the pole then reeling in the slack.

The fight lasted ten minutes, but eventually, the captain used a metal pole to pull the fish into the boat.

"Dude!" Isaiah said excitedly. "That was awesome." Isaiah and his brother high-fived, chest bumped and threw their fists into the air.

"Great job, man," Prince said, helping Joseph lift the fish in the air for a picture. "Get in here, Sal."

Smiling, I stood beside Prince as the captain took a picture. "Great catch Joseph," I said.

"Thanks. Now it's time for all of you to catch one," he said, baiting his hook and tossing his line back into the water.

"You won't catch two before I get my first, I promise you that," Isaiah said, rushing back to his side of the boat. Prince and I left our lines in the water and sat for a while.

"I was a small kid, smallest in my class until the summer of my sophomore year," Prince said. "I know it's hard to believe looking at me know, but I grew almost a foot that summer. Walked into school my junior year and everyone thought I was a *new* kid."

"Yeah, I would have had the same reaction. It must have hurt, right?" I asked, glancing over at Isaiah who was tying on more bait.

"It felt like my bones were going to come right through my skin," he said, rubbing his legs. "I was athletic too, but I couldn't do anything for weeks because it hurt so much. That's when I focused more on my singing."

I chuckled, remembering the story Mary-Ann told me. "Yeah, I heard you surprised your mother with a pretty significant part in Les Miserable on Broadway."

Prince looked up, smiling. "Who told you that?" he asked.

"Your mother. I asked her what her favorite memory was and…" He seemed shocked, almost disbelieving that performing on one of the biggest stages in the world, in one of the most iconic plays ever created, might not be worth remembering.

"How did your father die?" he asked, changing the subject.

"Pancreatic cancer. They caught it and treated it early, but it came back even stronger a few years later. Stage four at the age of seventy-two."

"I'm sorry to hear that. How long ago did it happen?" he asked.

"He fell into a coma and we decided to let his body decide eight years ago." The boat lifted, gliding over a wave.

"And your mother?" he asked, grabbing the railing.

"She took it pretty hard, but she's living with Mike on the upper east side and spends a lot of time with her quilting group and playing bingo.

Prince laughed, looking out across the water. "I don't see my father doing either of those things. But hopefully he'll find something."

"Your mother's not dead yet," I said, standing up and walking to my pole.

"I know," he said, standing as well. He reeled in his line to find the bait was gone. "But I feel for him. I mean, you were there the other day when she was losing it. Aaron told me that she threw her bedpan at him because she thought he was there to 'get' her."

"And after she got some rest, she sat calmly with him for over an hour whispering his name. She's still in there, Prince, and your father needs help remembering that." I felt my line get heavier. "I think I've got something," I said, pulling hard on the reel.

"Get it in, get it in," Isaiah said, rushing over.

If I hadn't taken a picture, no one, including myself would have believed I'd caught a six-foot blue shark. It took all four of us to keep it off the ground and the captain said it was one of only three he had landed in his boat. After a loud round of high-fives and a phone call to my brother, we tossed it back into the ocean.

By the end of the day, we caught another sailfish, and Isaiah caught a two-hundred-pound blue marlin. A catch worthy of a true fisherman.

We trolled back to the harbor with smiles glued to our lips and watched as the sun kissed the city goodnight.

"Thanks for inviting me," I said as I stepped out of Prince's car.

"Thank you for joining us. We had a great time." Prince stuck his hand out of the window, and I shook it. "My boys are leaving in the morning to get back for work, but I'll be in the city for a week. I'm sure I'll see you again before I head home."

"I'll be in touch," I said, walking to the trunk to grab my fish. "Nice meeting you guys," I said.

"Nice meeting you too, Sal." Isaiah and Joseph waved as they car rolled away.

After putting the fish into my freezer, I fell onto my bed, my arms sore and eyes heavy. Scout jumped up next to me, wagging his tail and rolling over onto his back. For the first time in a while. I fell asleep truly happy.

Chapter 10

"Have you been here long?" Prince asked as he approached. I was sitting in the chair outside Mary-Ann's room observing her as she sat by the window. She sang a hymn and rested her elbow on the sill, looking out at the park below.

"About thirty minutes," I said, closing my notepad and uncrossing my legs. "She's been sitting there the entire time." Mary-Ann was wrapped in a blue hospital blanket and her hair was tied up in the back. Her glasses sat on the end of her nose like a professor.

"Doing what?" he asked, taking the seat next to me.

"Nothing. Just looking out the window humming a song." I flipped my phone open to read a text Ryan sent me over an hour ago. I responded quickly and put my phone back into my pocket.

"You haven't gone in to see her?" Prince asked, pulling his left leg onto his knee.

"No, I was worried she might not recognize me and have another episode." I also wanted to take advantage of seeing her without anyone around. How she interacts with her environment and how she entertains herself when she was alone.

Prince exhaled, then stood. "I think I should go in," he said, looking down at me. I nodded and opened my notepad back up.

Prince approached slowly, his footsteps almost inaudible. "Mom," he said softly. "It's me, Prince."

Mary-Ann turned from the window and looked up at her son. Her eyes widened, and her mouth stretched into a lovely smile. The blanket that was draped over her shoulders fell off and landed on the floor. She was wearing a black shirt and a bead necklace that looked like a craft some of the children had made the week before.

"Prince," she said, reaching her arms out toward him.

Prince fell gently to his knees, wrapping his arms around his mother. Mary-Ann kissed him on the cheek and held his chin in her hands.

"It's good to see you mom," he said.

"Oh, it's lovely to see you too sweetheart." Her hands fell away from his face and she turned back to the window. "Sing with me, would you?"

She began, the words hard to hear from the hallway, but when Prince opened his mouth I was nearly brought to tears. *Amazing Grace, how sweet the sound. That save a wretch, like me.* He pulled the other chair next to her and sat. *I once was lost, but now I'm found. Was blind, but now I see.* I could tell why Mary-Ann's fondest memory was watching her son sing on Broadway. His voice was incredible. Mary-Ann looked back at Prince and smiled, her cheeks pinched, lips thinned to a straight line. Prince sang, his eyes locked on his mother's, Mary-Ann humming the harmony.

'Twas grace that taught my heart to fear, and grace my fears relieved. Mary-Ann turned and lay her head on Prince's shoulder. *How precious did that grace appear the hour I first believed.*

Prince laid his arm around his mother and swayed, the tree branches in the park joining their movement. As he sang the last verse, I walked in and sat quietly in the chair beside the door. *When we've been there ten thousand years, bright shining as the sun. We've no less days to sing God's praise, than when we'd first begun.*

"Thank you, baby," Mary-Ann said, patting Prince on the leg.

"I'm scared, mom."

Mary-Ann sat up. She shook her head slowly, wiping the few tears that fell from Prince's eyes. "You have nothing to fear Prince. God has his hand in yours and he's leading you to the promise land." Her smile inched back to her lips. Though

Prince would visit a number of times over the next year, that would be the last time Mary-Ann would ever call him by name, and one of the last times she would recognize him as her son.

"Who is that man?" Mary-Ann asked, pointing at me.

"That's my friend Sal. Sal Pitello." Prince looked back and shrugged.

"Is he a nice man?" Mary-Ann asked.

Prince got her blanket and put it on her lap. "He's one of the nicest men I've ever met. He's been writing a story about you."

Mary-Ann's lips opened to a circle, her head bouncing up and down. "Isn't that lovely. Tell him he should—" Mary-Ann paused. It began to rain, the droplets racing to the bottom of the window.

"Excuse me," a voice said from the door. We turned to find nurse Proctor standing with her hands in her pockets. "I'm here to take Mary-Ann to therapy." She walked in and stood at the foot of the bed.

"Mom, I'm going to go now, but I'll be back tomorrow okay?" Prince said, helping Mary-Ann into her wheelchair.

"Alright sweetheart."

"Nurse," I said as I stood. "I know that visitors aren't supposed to be here during a therapy session, but it would help if I could observe. For the story. It would help the reader better understand Mary-Ann's journey through the disease."

Nurse Proctor shook her head. "I can't do much about that. Our therapy sessions are normally very private."

"It will be like I'm not even there," I said with a smile.

"I'm sorry. There's paperwork that would need to be filled out by a family member, and you would need the permission of the therapist," she said, strapping Mary-Ann's legs in and pushing her toward the door.

"I'd be willing to fill out the paperwork," Prince said.

Nurse Proctor sighed. "Fine, but if doctor Imish says no, I don't want you trying to fight it." She pushed Mary-Ann into the hallway. "Mr. Pitello come with me. Mr. Cauldwell stop in with Nurse Benson and ask for the DH151 paperwork."

"Thank you," I said as Prince walked by.

The therapy room was three floors down in a room the size of half a basketball court. The wall at the far end was lined with mirrors and the floor was hardwood. A small desk sat in the corner next to the door, and chairs were stacked against the near wall. Nurse Proctor rolled Mary-Ann in and set her by the desk.

"Doctor Imish," she said, her voice echoing through the room.

Remember Me

A closet door opened and a short man in jeans, a button up shirt and glasses walked out holding a yoga ball. His skin was brown, and his beard hung down to the middle of his chest.

His voice was thick with a middle eastern accent. "Good afternoon, my love," he said, taking Mary-Ann's hands in his and spinning her around in a circle. Mary-Ann smiled widely. "And who is this?" he asked, looking at me.

"Mr. Pitello," I said, shaking his hand. "I'm a friend of the family, but more importantly, I'm writing a story about Mary-Ann and the effect this disease is having on her, her family and the community that supports her."

"Hmm." Dr. Imish stroked his beard. "What can I do for you?" he asked, walking to his desk.

"I told him that therapy sessions are supposed to be private, but he insisted, and Mary-Ann's son agreed to fill out the necessary paperwork." Nurse Proctor stepped to the desk and leaned forward, whispering something in Dr. Imish's ear.

"Having access to even one therapy session could help to better understand her progress," I said, pulling my bag off my shoulder and setting on the ground.

Doctor Imish thought for a long time, flipping through pages on a clipboard. "Thirty minutes. If you can stay out of my way, I will consider allowing you to stay longer or even come back for another session."

"Thank you, doctor," I said, picking up my bag and moving to the stack of chairs. Nurse Proctor smiled and waved before leaving.

Dr. Imish rolled out a mat and set up metal bars to help with walking. Mary-Ann struggled along the mat, grunting with each step. "One more step, that's it. One more," doctor Imish encouraged, his hand on her back helping to guide her. They spent ten minutes walking back and forth and sweat began to drip from Mary-Ann's face.

"Very good." Dr. Imish helped her into a beanbag chair. "Do you remember what we do next?" he asked, walking back to his desk. Mary-Ann took a slow drink from a plastic bottle and shrugged.

"Recognition," doctor Imish said, returning with a folder. "Your heart rate is up, so we must see how well your brain is working." He pulled a stack of photographs from the folder. Some were of Mary-Ann and her family, others were of fruits, cars and an assortment of other things found in the world. "Are you ready?" he asked, plopping down on the ground beside her.

Mary-Ann nodded her head and set the bottle down on the floor. "What is this?" he asked, holding up a picture of an apple.

"Fruit," Mary-Ann said with confidence.

"Good. What kind of fruit?"

Mary-Ann pointed at the picture, her hand gliding along the paper. "A... Apple." Doctor Imish placed the photo to his right and moved quickly to the next. "And this?"

"Another fruit. Allan loves these with his ice cream. That's a banana." Mary-Ann reached for her water bottle, knocking it over and spilling it onto the floor. "Oh, good heavens. Look what I've done."

"That's quite alright Mary-Ann," Dr. Imish said, hopping to his feet to get paper towels. He cleaned it quickly, then filled her bottle and returned to the floor. "What about his?" he said, holding up a picture of Aaron and his wife.

Mary-Ann snatched it from doctor Imish's hand and held it close to her face. "I know this man. I know this man. I know." Mary-Ann squeezed the picture in her hands and began to cry. "I know this man."

"That's right, you do. Who is he?" Dr. Imish said, not moving to comfort her. "This is your breakthrough. I don't want to give you the answer if I don't have to. You say you know that man, so tell me. Who is he?" Though his actions seemed distant and unemotional, his words were soft and pleasant.

"I can't remember his name. I love him. I know I love him. But I can't remember his name."

Mary-Ann struggle to look at the picture, each time breaking down even more.

"If you want me to help, all you have to do is ask. But only if you think you need it."

"I need it. You have to help me. I know this man. I know him." Mary-Ann thrust the picture back at him. He took it gracefully, flattening out the creases and set it down on the ground to his left. "He is one of your sons. His name is Aaron."

"Yes, yes!" Mary-Ann shouted with joy, shaking her fists in the air. "Aaron. My little Aaron and his wife. That's who it was."

"Only three left," doctor Imish said, holding up the next photograph. "Who is this?"

"He was a president." Mary-Ann stroked her chin in thought. "Lincoln."

"Correct. And this?" Dr. Imish held up a picture of the McDonald's golden arch.

"I can't say I enjoy eating there. It's far too greasy. McDonald's," she said, pointing her finger with certainty.

"This is the last one before we move on to the next activity, alright?" Dr. Imish said.

The picture was black and white. It was of Allan and her outside Full Bellies a few months after it opened. Mary-Ann was wearing a dressing spotted with flowers, white socks, and shoes with a strap that went over the top of her feet. Allan wore a pair of overalls, the left strap unhooked and hanging.

"Oh Allan," Mary-Ann said, taking the picture from Dr. Imish, this time more gently. "He sure loved those overalls." She hugged the photograph, then spun it around and pointed at the sign above their heads. "You know, he helped come up with the name. He came home from work one day and I was all strung up from being down at the church and I asked him what he wanted to eat, and you know what he told me?"

"What did he tell you?" Dr. Imish said, smiling beneath his beard.

"He told me, 'I don't care, just fill my belly,'" Mary-Ann giggled. She handed back the photo and exhaled. "That stuck in my head all the way to the next day. I told um...I told." Her lips quivered again, searching for Sharice's name. "Sharice. Yes, I told Sharice that if we are going to be feeding people, they ought to leave with their bellies full."

"That's wonderful Mary-Ann. You did a great job today." He placed the photographs back into the folder and walked to his desk.

Dr. Imish waved me over. "I think that will be all for you today. The next thing I must do involves movement while recognizing small objects. She has struggle in the past with this and I do not wish to put you in harm's way." He extended his hand.

"I appreciate you allowing me to sit in on one of your sessions," I said, shaking his hand.

"Pleasure. I will allow it again if you want. I can also update you on her progress at the end of each month if you think that will help."

"That would be great. Thank you," I said, slinging my bag over my shoulder. Mary-Ann smiled as I waved, her expression enough to say she was unsure of who I was.

Chapter 11

Thanksgiving 2009

"Turn that down, would you?" Prince said from upstairs. Aaron looked at me and laughed, turning the volume up two or three more notches. The New York Giants were playing the Denver Broncos for their Thanksgiving matchup. Aaron wore his 'lucky' Giants hat, signed by the 1991 Super Bowl MVP and star Giants running back, Ottis Anderson. I tried telling him the hat should be framed and never worn again, but his superstition seemed to play a huge role in that decision.

"Prince is just upset that they never play Oakland Raiders games," Aaron said, sliding the bowl of chips higher on his chest.

"I don't blame him. The Cincinnati Bengals are having a rough go at it too," I said as Denver scored their first touchdown.

Aaron threw his hands in the air and yelled, "Come on, play a little defense!" He twisted his hat to sit on his head backwards as if that would change the outcome.

"Bengals, huh. Why?" Aaron asked as the game went to a commercial.

"If I chose someone like the Giants, you and four million other people could, at any point, ask or tell me something about the team. Which would then put me in an embarrassing position because I really don't care that much about sports." I winked, feeling rather proud of myself.

"What about other Bengals fans?" Aaron sat up and placed the bowl of chips on the coffee table.

"I don't find that many around here, and I don't ever plan on being in Cincinnati, so I think I've got my bases covered."

Aaron laughed, wagging his index finger at me. "Clever."

"Oh no. Not a good start for your dwarfs, Aaron," Prince said with a laugh. He set a box down on the kitchen counter and grabbed a beer from the fridge.

"I'm not worried, it's only the first quarter."

Prince leaned against the wall. "You'll have to check the TVs at the laundromat across the street. We have to be at Full Bellies in thirty minutes for the unveiling. Thanksgiving dinner is right after, too." He took a sip of his beer and cringed as a Giants receiver fumbled after being hit from the side.

"I don't know how much more of this I can watch anyway," Aaron said. He leaned forward to tie his shoes. "You ready, Sal? Big day."

"Yeah, I think it will be nice," I said as I stood. Full Bellies had been closed off for the last week while Simeon Waldridge painted Malcolm on the mural. It took months to talk Katrina into doing it. She said it would be too much to see his face every time she went to work. But eventually, myself and the other women at the soup kitchen helped her understand the concept.

"He'll be lifted up by angels at the head of the march Kat," I had said, sitting in her living room having lunch.

"That will just be a reminder that he's dead." Katrina balled her fists and shook them, teeth clinched.

"Kat, don't take this as insensitive, but you don't need a picture of him on a mural to remember that he's gone. This will be a reminder that he's still here, watching over you and this community." I wrapped my arms around her and let her sob into my chest.

Prince shook me back to reality. "This is going to be pretty special."

We walked to the door and slipped on our coats. "I know, it's still hard to believe that just a few months ago Malcolm was happy, walking down the street to get money for the movies. The next second, he's gone." Prince and Aaron shook their heads in understanding as we walked onto the front porch.

The air bit the skin on my face and I turned away, walking backwards for a moment to break the wind. "It shouldn't be this cold in November," I said, squeezing the coat around my neck. "Who's picking up your mother?"

"Dad's on his way there now and the hospital is going to transport them," Aaron said as we climbed into the car.

I had watched Mary-Ann over the last several months quickly slip into stage five of Alzheimer's. Though she was still able to use the restroom independently, there was significant confusion and she struggled to recall even some of the simplest of details. Allan agreed to keep her in the Rehabilitation Ward but spent most of his time there with her.

"It will be nice for her to be out and about, don't you think?" I asked.

"Yep," Aaron said, toying with the radio. *And the Giants go into the second quarter down fourteen to nothing.*

"I tried to tell you Aaron, this is not their year," Prince said, making a left-hand turn. "You could turn that hat inside out and wear it as a shoe, and they still aren't going to win." I couldn't help but laugh, which resulted in a mean glance from Aaron.

When we arrived, the street was flooded with people in heavy jackets, gloves and winter hats. Katrina stood in the middle of the crowd. Maxine and Alise stood beside her and Sharice sat bundled in her wheelchair, a scarf around her neck making it difficult to see her face. I gave them each a hug and stood next to Kat, putting my arm around her waist and pulling her close to me.

"How are you feeling?" I ask, immediately regretting it. For years I've hated that question. To feel is such a personal emotion, not something that can be easily explained.

Kat looked over at me with a gentle expression and forced a smile. "I believe you when you say this will be good. I'm a little anxious to see what he's done, but there is some excitement there."

Smiling back, I said, "That's great to hear." I squeezed her again and a siren went off as an ambulance turned onto the street. "That must be Allan and Mary-Ann."

The door opened, and Mary-Ann was lowered to the ground in her wheelchair. Dozens of people clapped and shouted 'Mama,' as Allan rolled her over to us. "Almost didn't make it," Allan said, letting out a sigh of relief. "Nurse Benson and Dr. Imish had to be brought to her room just to convince her we weren't going to harm her. She nearly lost it again when she felt how cold it was, and there was an accident on ninety-second."

"But you're here," I said, clapping him on the back. He nodded his head and smiled, resituating his hat.

"Hello darling," Sharice said, leaning forward.

Allan bent forward and pointed. "Mary-Ann. Look, Sharice is here."

"Who?" she said, trying to follow his finger. Alise loosened the scarf around her mother's neck and it fell away from her face.

"Sharice, dear. Your best friend. The women that you opened Full Bellies with." Allan pointed again, sharing a compassionate smile.

"You know it was you that gave me the name for this place. Do you remember Allan. I went running in the next day to—" Mary-Ann paused and put a gloved finger to her chin. "What was I saying." Her hand fell back to her lap. "I'm sorry, I can't remember."

"It's alright honey," he whispered, rubbing her shoulders. "Where are Prince and Aaron?"

I shrugged my shoulders. "Maybe across the street watching the game. Although with how bad the Giants are playing, we may have heard Aaron yelling from over here."

Allan narrowed his brow. "You better watch what you say about the Giants." He snickered and punched me on the arm.

"Alright, alright," I laughed. "Oh, there's Prince," I said, pointing over by the building. "That's right, Simeon asked if they would help pull down the cover." Allan locked the wheels with his foot and asked if I would stand with Mary-Ann while he stepped away.

"I'm glad we are in the middle of all these people or I'd be frozen solid by now," I said. Katrina laughed in agreement. "It should only be a couple more minutes."

Simeon walked midway up a ladder and held a megaphone to his face. "I want to thank you all for coming out this afternoon for the reveal." The crowd cheered loudly, sending clouds of breath into the air. "When my father started this mural, I was eight years old. I knew that there was nothing else I wanted to do with my life than create, but I promised myself that I would only create things that truly meant something." I could feel Katrina shivering, though not from the cold.

"Although this addition is because of a loss, the loss of someone far too young, far too brave and someone that could have truly made a difference in this world. I know that with this, we can honor Malcolm and all the great things he would have done." More cheers rippled through the crowd.

"Kat," he said, the crowd turning their gaze to her. "We've known each other a long time. I hope that what I've done will bring a smile back to your face and begin to fill the emptiness that was left behind."

Simeon stepped down, set the megaphone aside, and stood in the middle of the covering. Grabbing it with both hands, Aaron, Simeon and Prince pulled away the tarp. The crowd lulled at a rumbling murmur as they looked at the wall. Katrina gently bounced up and down, tears pouring down her face.

Malcolm wore a black suit and red bowtie. He faced the other figures, a huge smile on his face as the faint outline of a pair of angels carried him into the clouds above. His arms were outstretched, and beneath his left arm read the words, *don't ever stop pushing forward.* It was remarkable. The crowd erupted, waving their hands and shouting 'Malcolm,' the echo dancing off the wind and carrying into the sky. Joining in, we hugged and soon, joy took over her tears.

As we settled, Aaron announced that the food was ready. The crowd moved aside as I pushed Mary-Ann toward the door. The room was lined with tables and chairs, leaf and turkey decorations hung from the ceiling, and the smell of cornbread and gravy attacked every inch of my nose.

"Do they need help in the kitchen?" Mary-Ann asked as I rolled her to the end of a table.

"I think they have everything under control," I said, unzipping her coat and pulling the gloves off her hands.

"Sharice doesn't want to sit at this table?" I asked Katrina, looking over at Alise who was locking her mother's wheels.

"She said it's too hard. She doesn't want all of this being her last memory of her best friend." Katrina unfolded a napkin and set in on Mary-Ann's lap.

"Who are you again?" Mary-Ann asked. "I know you, don't I?"

"Yes. I'm Sal Pitello. A friend of the family, and I'm writing a story about you." I smiled and held her hand.

"A story. That's wonderful. Did I ever tell you about how this place got its name?" Her face brightened, her smile filling her lips.

"Yes, you have," I said, squeezing her hands gently, then letting them fall onto her lap.

"I have what?" she said, tilting her head sideways.

Katrina made quick eye contact with me and frowned, looking back at Sharice. "I'm going to get you a plate," I said, walking to the counter.

Mary-Ann sat quietly for most of the evening, conversations spiraling around her and the noise in the room crashing in like waves.

170

Katrina found me much later. She threw her arms around my neck and thanked me for all my support. I offered to walk her home, a four-block trek in the freezing cold. When we arrived at her apartment, we parted ways with a kiss and, at least for me, a smile that stuck to my lips even after I closed my eyes to sleep.

Chapter 12

December 2009

With Mary-Ann's condition, I cancelled my trip to Florida, telling my sister I would try again in the summer.

Colorful lights and decorations filled the Rehabilitation Ward, making it a Christmas wonderland. The yellow brick road was painted red, green and white. Santa and his reindeer took up most of the wall in the main hallway. Paper snowflakes hung from the ceiling. Several children skipped between rooms dropping off freshly baked sugar cookies cut in different shapes.

I waved to Nurse Benson, signed in and walked to Mary-Ann's room. The door was open when I arrived, and I could hear the faintest of giggles coming from inside. I took the seat outside of the room and watched as Mary-Ann sat by the window, a pair of scissors in her hands, cutting her own snowflake.

A little boy sucking a lollipop sat next to her. He wore a red sweatshirt, black shorts and a pair of white Nikes on his feet. On his head was a blue hat pulled down over his ears. It was then I realized it was the boy that had given her a hug in the park so many months ago. I couldn't hear what they were saying, but their laughter filled the room every so often as small pieces of paper fell to the ground. I moved the chair slowly to the edge of the doorway.

"I used to make these with my children," Mary-Ann said, setting the scissors down on the windowsill and unfolding her snowflake.

"Wow," the boy said, twisting his body to get a better look. He spun upside down, his tongue falling out of his mouth.

"Oh, you stop that," Mary-Ann giggled, tickling him on the neck. "Where should I put this?" she asked. The boy pointed at the window, just above his head. "Tear off some of that tape and hand it here." Mary-Ann demonstrated how to make a loop with the tape, so you could stick it to the back. He helped her secure it to the window and they sat back in their chairs, their faces oozing with satisfaction. "Remind me of your name. I think I've forgotten," Mary-Ann said.

"Again," the boy sighed, shaking his head in confusion. "My name is Landon. Landon, Landon, Landon. My full name is Landon Patrick Seawith. I was born on May fifth to my parents Sherry and Michael. My mother is a nurse here at the hospital and my dad works as a building manager for schools. He says that—"

"Slow down, slow," Mary-Ann said, gesturing with her hands. "I've almost forgotten your name again with all that talking."

"We should make name tags, that way you won't ever forget." Landon's smile grew, baring a missing tooth on the left side of his mouth.

"That is a wonderful idea." Mary-Ann looked out the window. Snow fell gently from the sky, piling up on the ground below. "Tell me why you're here again," she said, turning her attention back to Landon.

"I like to say a monster climbed in through my ear and started eating away at my brain. But, my mom says that I shouldn't tell people that." He reached for his head and pulled away his hat. His head was bald, thin ripples of blue and red veins running along his scalp like rivers on a map.

"A monster?" Mary-Ann gasped, holding her hands over her mouth. "What kind of monster?"

"Its name is cancer. It's the third time it's come back." He turned his head to show her the scar that ran along the back. "The first time was when I was four. The doctors said if I survived the surgery, it was likely the cancer would return. And it did. Two years later they tried to cut it all out again." Landon slipped his hat back over his head and crossed his arms. "'He's a strong kid.' That's what all the doctors and nurses keep saying." Uncrossing his arms, he raised his right arm and flexed, pulling the sleeve up to make his arm look bigger.

"Oh my, you are strong. Look at that," Mary-Ann said. She reached out and grabbed his arm, pulling him in close and tickling his armpit. Landon rolled free, his breath heavy and mouth spilling with drool.

"That's my most ticklish spot," he pouted, trying to catch his breath. He couldn't stay upset very long, his arms crossed over his chest and a smile creeping back to his lips.

I heard footsteps from down the hallway and turned to find Allan walking up with a vase of flowers and a small box of chocolates. He smiled and waved. "Hey, I didn't know you were coming today. How is she doing?" he said, stopping at my side and considering the room. "Hey, what—"

I grabbed him by the arm and held my finger up to my lips to silence him. "Just watch," I whispered.

"I'm almost ten now and this time, the doctor said he hopes it won't ever come back. I can't ever play football though. I really love football, but I wouldn't be able to handle all the contact." Landon rolled his sleeves up to his elbows to show Mary-Ann another scar. "This happened when I was walking through the kitchen. I wasn't looking where I was going and walked into the side of the table."

Mary-Ann let her lips fall to a frown, then leaned down and kissed his arm. "Poor thing, what happened?"

"I just told you I walked into a table," Landon said with a laugh.

"Yes, of course. Remind me of your name sweetheart."

Landon exhaled audibly and stood. "I'll be back. I'm going to go ask Nurse Benson for paper so I can make a name tag." He turned and bolted for the door, dodging between Allan and me as if he didn't care that we were there.

Allan walked into the room and set the chocolates down on the bed. "Hello, love," he said, taking the seat next his wife.

"Allan. I'm so glad you're here. I've just met this nice young boy, but I can't remember his name." Mary-Ann searched the room for him. "He was just here, I swear it." She was growing agitated, her hands stiffening into fists.

"He will be right back. Don't worry." Allan stroked her back and she calmed, looking out the window at the falling snow. The tree branches were bare, and you could see the buildings that sat on the other side of the park.

"Look, I've brought you some flowers." Allan set the vase down on the windowsill.

"They're beautiful Allan. Thank you. Amaryllis too, they're my favorite." She leaned forward and sniffed the pedals. "Lovely," she said, hugging herself.

"Nurse Benson said to be careful with the scissors Mama," Landon said as he walked back into the room. "Hey mister." He looked Allan up and down, then dropped a handful of materials onto a small table. "My name is Landon. Landon Patrick Seawith. I'm going to make a name tag, so Mama won't forget."

"That's a clever idea. Would you like me to help?" Allan asked.

"No, I've got this. I will need you to move when I'm done though. I *was* sitting there." Without hesitating, Landon went to work on his nametag. Allan shot a funny look my way.

"There we go," Landon said, pulling the tag off the back and sticking his name on his chest. "I wrote my entire name, see. Landon Patrick Seawith, but you can just call me Landon."

Mary-Ann turned and clapped her hands together. "Allan, this is the boy I was telling you about. His name is—"

"Landon Patrick Seawith. I know, we've just met," Allan interrupted sarcastically. Instead of making a fuss, Allan stood up from his seat.

"Thanks mister," Landon said, quick to move in.

"I also brought you some chocolates, love," Allan said, getting the box off the bed and setting them on her lap.

"Thank you. Are you going somewhere?" she asked.

"Just over here to this chair." Allan sat just inside the room. "Quite the kid huh?" he asked.

"Yeah. Smart. I think he might be good for her you know." I closed my notepad and placed it on the ground beside me.

"How so?" he asked.

"Well, he doesn't have much concept of the disease and he seems to push past the frustration of her forgetting things. Maybe it would be good for her to spend time with him." I crossed a leg over my knee and folded my arms. "I don't know. Just a thought."

"Yeah and next thing you know, he's pushing her all around the hospital. I don't think so." Allan looked back at his wife who was smiling, listening to Landon tell a story.

"I'm sure the nurses could keep a close eye on their movement," I said hopefully.

"Well it doesn't look like anyone is keep an eye on either of them right now," he responded. "Who is he anyway, and why is he just allowed to be in the room."

With a smirk I said, "His name is Landon. Landon Patrick Seawith."

"Ah, shut up," Allan spat, a twinkle of a smile gracing his lips.

Just then, Nurse Proctor walked up carrying a small plate of fruit. "Hello gentlemen. I see you've met our newest couple, Landon and Mary-Ann." She smiled and walked into the room, placing the fruit on the small table.

"Thank you, Ms. Proctor," Landon said, reaching over and snatching up a few grapes.

"You are most welcome, Little Superman," she said as she walked back toward the door.

"What do you mean new couple?" Allan asked. "Why haven't I been told they were spending so much time together?"

"I could hardly believe you should be worried Mr. Cauldwell. The boy is only nine years old." Nurse Proctor leaned against the doorway, one hand stuffed into a pocket. "Anyway, we found Landon about a week ago putting together a puzzle and talking to her while she was taking a nap. We didn't see any harm in it and reported to Dr. Imish. He said, 'a bit of young energy might actually be good for her.'"

"It still doesn't explain why I wasn't—"

"Allan," I said, resting my hand on his shoulder. "I think they were worried you might overreact. Now I know I'm not your son, but I think

I've gained some respect over the last year and half, right?" Allan nodded his head. "Then believe me when I say you are overreacting. Let's just see how this all plays out."

"Watch this," Landon said. We looked over as Landon was tossing a grape in the air. It fell cleanly into his mouth and he bowed like an Olympic gymnast.

"Well done, Landon," Mary-Ann said, clapping her hands. "Try another."

Landon reached back to the plate and grabbed the last two grapes. "I'll throw it even higher this time okay?" The grape nearly hit the ceiling and came crashing down into Landon's cheek.

Mary-Ann burst with laughter and I heard her snort for the first time. I glanced over at Allan, his eyes wide and filling with tears. I could tell it was the first time he had heard it in a long time. Squeezing his shoulder, I mouthed the word, 'see,' and smiled. Their laughter went on for several minutes.

Before leaving, Allan invited me to the Christmas party at the hospital at the end of the week. "It will be fun," he said with a shake of my hand.

◇

Gabriel Fowler

The lights flashed to the sound of *Jingle Bell Rock*. Doctors and nurses alike were dressed in ugly sweaters. The patients sat in a circle in the main lobby for a round of *white elephant*. Christmas presents were piled high in the middle, the smell of warm apple cider floating through the air.

I sat off to the side and watched as some of the children poked at presents and family members piled in for an evening of celebration.

Allan sat beside Mary-Ann, his arm resting gently on her leg. He wore clip on elf ears and a green hat, his smile breaking easily through his lips. Landon sat on the floor between Mary-Ann's legs; his parents, sat on the other side. He collapsed his fingers together and looked at the pile with eager eyes.

"Can I have everyone's attention please," Nurse Benson said as he climbed onto a chair.

His sweater was dark brown with strips of real bark glued to the chest and arms. A cardboard cutout of a squirrel rested on his shoulder, its cheeks plump with acorns. The room settled save for the occasional child giggling. "Thank you for coming out this evening. We have the pleasure of hosting the annual white elephant gathering and hope everyone leaves very unhappy with their gift."

The room bounced with laughter. Nurse Benson raised his hand to quiet them before continuing. "There are plenty of snacks on the table

181

in the corner, as well as drinks, so don't be bashful. Without further ado, let's get this thing started." He raised his fist into the air and shouted, sending excitement through the room.

A girl of seven battling seizures was the first to choose her present. Dozens of little hands pointed all around the pile trying to convince her which one to choose. A small blue box with a white bow caught her eye and she snatched it into her hands. As she opened the box, it was hard to see as every child rushed to look over her shoulder. Confused, the girl raised the gift into the air and said, "What is it?" Her mother, a plump blonde wearing jeans and a white sweater giggled, pulling her daughter close and whispering in her ear. "Ew. I don't want this," she said, throwing a small box of Q-tips on the ground.

"It's alright Mikenzi," Nurse Benson said. "Hold onto the gift because you will have a chance at the end to steal anyone else's gift you might want." Though reluctant, she knelt and picked up the Q-tips before finding a seat on her mother's lap.

In ten minutes, we saw a toy car, chocolate (which was stolen), a gift card to Starbucks, a flashlight and a bar of soap. Having never seen or played this game, I was at the edge of my seat after each number was called and a new present was being opened. I made a quick note to make sure I mention it to my brother for our Christmas party a few weeks later.

"Number sixteen," Nurse Benson said as the room quieted.

"That's you," Landon said, turning to face Mary-Ann. "I can get your present for you. You just need to tell me which one you want." Landon stood and placed his hands on Mary-Ann's knees, leaning in close to her face.

"I can't see the pile if you're standing there, now can I?" Mary-Ann crunched her nose and stuck her tongue out at him. He jumped to the side. His mother grabbed him by the waist and pulled him in for a hug. "That one, there," Mary-Ann said, pointing.

Landon wriggled free and lunged toward the pile grabbing a large black box. "This one?" he asked, barely able to lift it.

"No, that one." Landon moved to a smaller, yellow box but Mary-Ann shook her head. "Not that one, the bag next to it with tissue paper coming out." Landon hurried back with the bag and set it down on her lap.

Mary-Ann slowly pulled out the tissue paper. Inside was a round, heavy ball covered in green and red wrapping paper. Her hands shook, and her nails were too brittle as she tried to tear the paper free.

"I can help if you'd like," Landon said. Mary-Ann gladly handed it over, watching as Landon tore the paper off and handed back a snow globe of New York City. "So cool," Landon said, jumping up and down. "Hey everyone, look. It's a snow globe. Did you know that the grandson of Erwin Perzy, an Austrian man, invented these back in 1905?"

Landon seemed to miss the shocked stares that waved through the room, turning back and admiring the flakes of snow as they fell over the Empire State Building. "No one better steal this from Mama. It's good luck. It will help her remember." He looked up at Mary-Ann with an expression only a child could, eyes gentle, cheeks dimpled and mouth agape with glaring white teeth.

"It really is beautiful. What did you say this was?" Mary-Ann asked.

"It's a snow globe, sweetheart," Allan said, reaching over and giving it a shake. "See, all the snow is falling over New York."

"How wonderful. This will go right on the windowsill next to the—" Her eyes wandered back to the pile of presents, forgetting and remembering all in one.

By the end of the evening, the pile of presents turned into a giant pile of wrapping paper and empty gift bags. Landon came away with a candle, which he wasn't too upset about, saying,

'It's supposed to smell like strawberries. I love strawberries.' He continued to protect Mary-Ann and her snow globe every time someone walked by looking for a present to steal.

Mikenzi ended up trading her Q-tips for a bag of peanut M&Ms, falling into her mother's lap with a far more pleasant look on her face.

"That was quite the game," I said to Nurse Benson as I helped clean.

"You've never played?" he asked, tossing a plate of half-eaten cookies into the trash.

"Never even heard of it. That's something my family and the office needs to do."

"It can get a little crazy when a few drinks are involved." He opened another trash bag and I pushed an arm full of wrapping paper to the bottom. "Thanks for helping clean up. That means a lot."

"Of course. Allan's helping Mary-Ann into bed and I told him I'd ride the train back with him. I wasn't going to just sit here and watch."

"They don't all come like you. Some of the parents leave fifteen minutes early just so they don't have to." He laughed, taking a bottle and spraying the table with it.

"I can't say I would have always done it. After meeting the Cauldwell family, I feel like I'm a completely different person, and better for it." I helped wipe down the table and walked to the front desk when we were finished.

"You ready?" a voice said from behind me. Turning, I found Allan with a small basket of cookies in his hands and a grin on his face.

"I'm ready. Have a good night, Nurse Benson," I said, knocking my knuckles on the counter and heading for the door.

"You too, fellas," he said.

Allan fell into the train seat with a thump, the smile still glued to his lips. "That was really nice," he said, setting the basket to the side and turning to face me. "I think that kid really will be good for her. She hasn't had an outburst in two weeks and she's getting her smile back." Allan's head fell onto the window.

"What did I say? Young energy."

"I didn't believe it at first, but you were right. Thanks for coming out tonight."

"Of course."

Allan sat forward, his elbows resting on his knees. "God knows I have enough, but you're like a son to me now, you know that right?" He turned his head and smiled a different smile, a fatherly smile. "If there's anything I can ever do, don't hesitate to ask."

Chapter 13

Almost two weeks in and the new year had come and gone, leaving behind the remnants of cheers from a boisterous crowd bundled in their winter jackets watching the ball drop in Time Square. Road cleaners and garbage men scoured the city, cleaning what was left of broken bottles and confetti bombs, New York, fading back into an assembly line of gears working to keep the lights on. A few inches of snow still stuck to the cold, hard ground. Kicking my boots off on the outer brick wall, I shivered walking into the hospital.

"Back again, Mr. Pitello?" one of the nurses at the main desk asked. She was a fair-skinned brunette with long fingernails and lipstick brighter than the sun. A pleasant woman but I came to learn she was recently divorced and looking to 'test the waters' once again.

"Yes, Ms. Childress. The stories not going to write itself," I said, throwing a friendly smile her way.

"Oh, call me Debby." She fluttered her eyes awkwardly, twisting her hair with a finger like a 70s teen from California. "I had an idea. Why don't you come by my place, we'll have a glass of wine and we can read through that book of yours. You know, make some edits." Speechless, I fidgeted with my bag and rushed to the elevator.

As my feet landed in the Rehabilitation Ward, a sense of calm waved over me. "Morning Nurse Benson," I said, quickly signing in and headed to Mary-Ann's room. Only the white glow from the window lit the room, sending thin rays of light through the blinds. The bed was empty, blankets tossed to the side and one of the railings hung down below the mattress. Mary-Ann's snow globe sat on the windowsill, the flecks of snow spread evenly across the floor of New York, much like it was outside. I pulled the blind to the side and peer out at the small park. Mary-Ann and Landon lay on their backs, arms and legs waving back and forth. I quietly opening the window and I could hear laughter. Allan sat on the bench, Mary-Ann's empty wheelchair beside him.

"Let's stand up and see what they look like," Landon shouted, throwing a handful of snow in the air. He jumped up quickly, thrusting his arms above his head.

Allan helped Mary-Ann to her feet, brushing the snow from her back. "Oh, they looked wonderful," Mary-Ann said.

"Way cool. Did you know that the world record for most snow angels made simultaneously in a single place is 8,962 in North Dakota? It happened only a couple years ago on the State Capitol Grounds in Bismarck." Landon squatted, rolled up a handful of snow and threw it.

"How do you know so much?" Allan asked, helping Mary-Ann back into her wheelchair.

Landon shrugged. "I just remember something that I read, or see, or something someone tells me. I love learning new things."

"It's quite remarkable." Allan sat back down and blew hot air into his hands.

"I'm going to build a snowman." Landon rushed into the opening and slid on his knees. His hands worked quickly forming a small snowball. He then began the process of rolling it over and over until it was too heavy for him to push. "That will be the base," he said. I closed the window and made my way down to the park, the cold air seeping through my clothes and jackhammering at my bones. Allan saw me from afar and waved me over, his eyes grinning beneath his scarf.

"Good morning, Sal," he said.

"Good morning, everyone." I looked out at Landon who was rolling the body and gave him a thumbs-up. He smiled, focusing all his energy back to the snow. "I love what you've done with the place Mama," I said, planting a kiss on her cheek. "Your snow angels look amazing." Mary-Ann waved at the ground, her lips parting, struggling to find words.

"Hey mister," Landon said. "Could you help me lift this onto the base?"

Patting Mary-Ann gently on the arm, I trudged through the snow to where Landon was standing. "Get started on the head and I'll bring this over," I said, bending down and wrapping my arms around the boulder.

Landon scurried off and quickly returned with a third, but smaller and more lopsided snowball. After placing it on top, we went about forming the spheres, stuffing excess snow into the cracks to keep it sturdy.

"Perfect," Landon said with excitement, punching the air. "I'll go get some stones for the eyes and buttons and sticks for his arm." As he ran off, he shouted, "You're on carrot duty."

Giggling, I walked back to the bench. "Where am I going to find a carrot out here?" I asked, crossing my arms.

Allan laughed. "You better find something, or that kid's going to be rather disappointed." He pushed me away, throwing a small handful of snow.

"Thanks a lot." Looking back, I could see his face crinkled.

"It's not a carrot, but it will have to do," I said, returning with a short, fat stick.

"And, there. Perfect." Landon stepped back, waving his arms like an artist presenting their masterpiece.

"Looks great," I said, holding my hand up.

He slapped it and said, "Thanks mister."

"Sal," I said with a smile.

"Is that short for Salvador?" he asked as he sat down on the bench in between Mary-Ann and Allan. He brushed the snow off his legs.

"Yes, my full name is Salvador Louise Pitello."

"Were you named after the artist?" Landon asked.

I bent down and grabbed a handful of snow, rolling it around in my hands. "Salvador Dali?"

"Salvador Felipe Jacinto Dali y Domenech, to be exact." Landon scooched back on the bench, resting his arm on Mary-Ann's wheelchair. "My mother has a replica of The Persistence of Memory. You know, his 1931 painting of the melting clocks."

I stood baffled at the nonchalance of his knowledge, his ability to remember. It was as if there was a transfer of power between him and Mary-Ann, a connection they weren't even aware of.

"I know that painting. It's probably the only one I'd recognize."

The door to the hospital opened and Nurse Proctor stepped out. "It's time to come back inside. We don't want either of you staying out too long and getting sick, okay?" She waved, stepping back behind the glass.

Landon hopped to his feet and spun the wheelchair. He was barely able to see over the top, but he pushed, grunting with each step.

"Almost there," Mary-Ann said.

Allan took over as we went through the door, kicking the snow from his boots. "Let's get you out of your wet clothing alright," Nurse Proctor said, pulling the hat off Landon's head. "There's a cup of hot cocoa waiting for you." She leaned down and whispered loudly into his ear. "With extra marshmallows."

"Yes!" Landon jumped up and down. "Did you hear that," he said, planting a kiss on Mary-Ann's cheek. "Hot cocoa with extra marshmallows."

"That will warm us right up," she said, reaching for her scarf.

We sat on a couch in the main lobby, our hands clamped tightly around our cups, steam twisting up like the smoke from a campfire.

"There are so many marshmallows I can't even see the hot cocoa," Landon said, poking at them with his finger. "Mama. Do you want to play a game?" he asked.

"I think I'm too tired for games after all that fun in the snow." Mary-Ann's hands shook as she lifted her cup to her lips.

"But this game is simple. It's all about creating a story and using strategy. It's called *Find the Buried Treasure.*"

"I've never heard of that game before," Mary-Ann said. Her eyelids were heavy, slowly dropping closed as her head tilted forward.

"It's so much fun!" Landon shouted, bouncing in his seat and jarring Mary-Ann's eyes open.

Allan looked on with concern. "Maybe the two of you can play another time. She needs her rest."

"Okay," Landon said, tossing a marshmallow into his mouth and chewing happily. "I can't wait!" He slid off the couch, nearly spilling his drink. "Bye Mama. Bye Mr. Cauldwell. Bye Salvador." With a wave, he was gone, skipping down the hallway, droplets of hot cocoa leaving a trail behind him. I helped Allan get Mary-Ann into her bed before heading to the office.

◇

"Where are you off to so quickly Domonique?" I asked, throwing my bag on Ryan's desk.

"Haiti," she said as she stuffed her lenses into her camera bag. "You didn't hear? Major earthquake, millions homeless in a matter of minutes."

I stared blankly at the television on the wall. Bodies were scattered across rubble filled streets, crying mothers cradling their dead children. A rescue crew worked vigorously alongside locals to find survivors. "I had no idea. When did this happen?" I asked, taking my phone from my pocket. Four missed calls and three emails. "Damn. Sorry Ryan, I was at the hospital with Mary-Ann."

"It's fine. I put our new hires to work on the phones and Domonique is leaving with Collin on the next flight out. We've got things covered." He rolled his chair to the end of his desk and grabbed a piece of paper off the top of a stack. "Amy said this needs a fact check. The woman at the construction site said to call for a follow-up interview. Other than that, it's ready for print."

"Alright. I'll make a few phone calls now and get it back to you. Are you sure there's nothing I can do about this Haitian thing?"

"Not unless you want to get on a plane and go there," Ryan said, looking up at Domonique.

"It's not that I don't like Collin. He just thinks he's a smooth talker, but really, he sounds like a horse that's desperate for water." Domonique zipped up her camera bag and slung it over a shoulder.

Ryan shrugged. "Is that a good enough reason for you to go Sal?" he asked, sarcasm seeping through every word.

"As much as I love you Dom, you're a strong enough woman to fight off the likes of Collin." I rested a compassionate hand on her shoulder and walked to my office.

Chapter 14

February 2010

Super Bowl Forty-Four. I sat in Allan's living room pinched between Aaron and Prince on the loveseat, their legs hanging over the armrests. Isaiah and Joseph were back in town, along with Carol, Paul and all the wives. Allan sat on a folding chair, his legs propped up on the coffee table.

"Ten bucks the Colts win by thirty," Prince said, taking a bite of a hamburger.

"No way, Dad," Joseph said, lying on the floor with his chin resting in his hands. "Drew Brees is a beast. Saints win by at least a touchdown."

"Who wants another hamburger before I leave?" Carol asked from the kitchen. A few hands went to the air and she collected their plates. "There you go," she said, handing the plates back and wiping her hands on the apron tied around her waist.

"Give Mama our love," Aaron said.

Gabriel Fowler

Carol removed the apron and hung it on the wall. "I will. Enjoy the game everybody."

"Thank you," we all said, waving as she exited the house.

"Everyone remembers the rule, right?" Joseph said, sitting up and looking around the room.

Confused, I turned and shook my head. "The rule?"

"Yeah. This dummy won a bet four years ago that he could eat an entire medium pizza, a side of garlic *and* cinnamon bread sticks all by himself," Prince said. "Only my son would do something so stupid." The room rumbled with laughter.

Joseph went to his knees, throwing his arms out to the side. "That's what you get for challenging me."

"What did you win?" I asked, still uncertain.

"I said he could have anything he wanted, within reason. You'd think a mid-twenties, single guy trying to figure out what he wants to do with his life would choose something like, I don't know, money. A new car. A trip somewhere. Nope. He said he wanted to create a rule for our annual Super Bowl Party. No one is allowed to talk during the commercials." Prince shook his head in shame.

"What?" I said, even more confused than before.

"Yup. Not a word. The game is good and all, but the commercials are what the night is really

197

about." Joseph laid back down, a sense of accomplishment rolling of his back.

"You should have invited Katrina," Elizabeth said as the game started. She sat on the floor beneath Prince, a blue ribbon tied in her hair and a blue sequined shirt to match.

"I asked. She said she had plans with some of the ladies from the soup kitchen."

Elizabeth nodded her head. "Prince tells me things have been moving forward with you two."

"Yes, but very, very slowly. I'm extremely busy at the office and at the hospital with Mary-Ann. It doesn't leave a lot of time to be social." Aaron accidentally bumped my arm as a pass was intercepted.

"I see. Well, Kat is a wonderful woman. Don't wait too long." Elizabeth smiled and turned back to the television.

As the game progressed, the room was, aside from commercials, at a constant volume of ten. I even found myself shouting at the screen when there was a missed tackle or dropped pass. New Orleans ended the second quarter down four and we quickly dispersed throughout the house, uninterested in, The Who's, halftime performance.

"I tried to tell you," Prince said, standing by the kitchen table snacking on a bowl of potato chips. "The Saints just don't have an answer. They don't have a star player that's going to put them at the next level."

"Two words dad. Drew...Brees," Joseph said, taking a can of soda from the fridge.

"I'm starting to agree with your father," Aaron jumped in. "Drew Brees is good, but this is a big game and the guys under six feet tall. I don't know how he's going to handle the pressure."

"Just wait and see." Joseph flipped the can through the air and caught it as he walked back into the living room to find his seat.

"Oh!" Joseph shouted, jumping to his feet at the start of the second half. "I told you."

"They may have recovered the onside kick, which is one of the riskiest plays I've seen in a Super Bowl. But now they have to capitalize," Isaiah said.

New Orleans took the lead after a Pierre Thomas touchdown reception and the house began to shake. Joseph threw himself into the air, landing with a resounding thud and running around the room looking for high-fives.

"If my house falls down, I'm going to whoop that black ass of yours," Allan said, wagging a finger. His mouth flew open and his laugh shot out like a cannon. The look on Joseph's face was enough to get the entire room rolling, tears streaming down each of our faces.

Although the Colts retook the lead, New Orleans outscored them eighteen to nothing the rest of the game to win 31-17. "I should have put money on this game," Joseph said. "Drew Brees with 32 of 39 completions for 288 yards and two touchdowns. Easily the MVP." He walked over to his father and leaned forward, though putting himself in a position to run quickly if he needed to. "You don't say it often, but I want to hear it. 'Son, you were right.'" Joseph put his hand to his ear to make sure he heard every word.

"You were right," Prince whispered.

"Sorry, what? I'm not sure if I heard you."

"Boy you better—" Prince sprung from his seat, Joseph squealing as he tried to get away. We watched as they ran around the coffee table. Joseph eventually gave up, curling into a ball on the floor and shouting 'mercy' as Prince jabbed at his ribs. Exhausted, but with a smile on my face, I said my farewells and headed home.

◇

"You look tired," Katrina said as I walked into the kitchen. The other women were already halfway through lunch preparations and the room smelled of boiled noodles and freshly chopped onions. "Did you have fun watching the game?"

"I did. That family knows how to have a good time." I gave her a hug and reached under the counter for a pair of plastic gloves.

Katrina was slowly working her way back into a routine, spending a few days at Full Bellies and at least a day with Alise helping look after her mother. Monday's were easier for her, the church service from the day before boosting her spirit and allowing her to believe there was a light at the end of the tunnel.

"How's Mary-Ann doing?" she asked, opening a box of elbow noodles and dumping them in a pot.

"Better, and worse. It's hard to tell," I said, peeling an onion.

"How so?"

"Well, the doctors say her brain is continuing to deteriorate. She's forgetting more and more. At this point the only face she really remembers is Allan's and she struggles to remember him occasionally. But, there's this boy." I tossed the onion into a bowl and started on another.

"Allan mentioned something a few Sundays ago about a boy she's been spending time with, but I wasn't paying that much attention."

"Landon Patrick Seawith. And the only reason I know his full name is because he has a habit of saying it several times. One of the smartest nine-year-olds I've ever met. His memory is remarkable."

Some of the ladies began to sing, their voices like an angelic church choir. *Swing low. Sweet chariot. God's gonna trouble, the water.*

"Go on, girl. Hit that low note," a woman said. "Sound like someone hit you in the gut and you struggling to get the air out." The others laughed, waving their towels around their heads.

"Why is he there?" Katrina asked, looking over her shoulder and smiling at the women.

"Brain cancer. He's had three surgeries so far."

"Poor thing."

"Yeah. But when those two are together, it's like Mary-Ann is young again. They made snow angels the other week, they play cards, do crafts together. It's like he has a superpower or something." My pile of onions was peeled, so I wiped down the cutting board and began dicing them with a knife.

"It wouldn't be that unbelievable if she were feeding off of his energy," Katrina said.

"That's exactly what I told Allan. He was worried at first, but he seems pretty happy with the 'relationship.'" I nudged her with my elbow, and I could see her eyes rolled into the back of her head.

"Come on now, we're trying to work." she said, swiping an elbow back in my direction.

"You're damn right we are." I bumped her with my hip, sending her into the sink behind me. She gasped, grabbed a handful of water and threw it at me. With water dripping from my face, I set the knife down, an evil smile clinging to my lips. For a moment, it felt like we were alone at the age of fifteen. I chased her around the kitchen with a wet towel. Her giggle cascaded from her mouth, bouncing off the countertop and pouring onto the floor. The sound of the room slowly came back as we stood panting, smiles still pulled to our cheeks. We stared at the other women in silence, their expressions twisted.

"Just get a room already," Maxine said, twirling her towel around her head. Laughter bubbled and burst around the room. Embarrassed, Katrina sauntered back to where she had been working.

As the lunch crowd piled in, I pulled Kat to the side. "I didn't mean for you to get upset. I just really enjoy being around you."

"No Sal. It's not you. You're great, but it's hard for me to smile and laugh sometimes. It feels like I'm betraying him in some way."

"I get that. But eventually you have to realize that he would want you to be happy." I smiled, pulling on her elbow and landing a gentle kiss on her cheek. "Come to dinner with me tonight."

She hesitated, her arms falling weightless at her sides. "Fine. But nothing fancy. I'm not that kind of girl."

"Deal. Waffle House it is."

"Perfect."

"Wait really? I was only kidding." I raised my eyebrows.

"Nope. That's exactly what I want." She went back to the kitchen without another word.

Chapter 15

April 2010

Most of the snow melted away leaving small puddles of water all around the city. Work in the office was slow and I only had a week left until Amy needed my three-page spread for the May release; so, I hopped on the train and headed to the hospital.

Mary-Ann's room smelled of lavender, a small candle flickering on her bedside table. She sat in her wheelchair with her back to the window, an eyepatch over her right eye and brown marker drawn all over her chin. Landon sat on the bed across from her, a paper hat resting on his head and a stuffed bird tied to his shoulder. Taking the seat by the door, I opened my notepad and blended into the background, letting the scene unfold.

"So what kind of treasure are we going to be looking for?" Landon asked, trying to sound like a pirate.

Mary-Ann giggled, holding her hand over her mouth and shrugging her shoulders. "Well, I don't know. Something shiny I guess." She clapped her hands together as she smiled her famous smile.

"Jewels and gold and silver eh?" Landon raised his hand above his head, thrusting a paper sword into the air. "Okay, now we need to name our ship. Some of the most famous names for pirate ships are Roebuck, Queen Anne's Revenge and The Black Pearl. But I think we should come up with our own. Something clever eh," he said, giggling every time he said 'eh.'

"What did you have in mind?" Mary-Ann asked, gingerly scratching her face.

"Hmm. How about… Mary-Ann's Delight. What do you think Craggy?" he said, turning to his bird. *Mary-Ann's Delight. Mary-Ann's Delight,* the bird squawked.

"That settles it. We are pirates, sailing the seven seas on board our vessel, Mary-Ann's Delight. In search of buried gold, silver and jewels."

"Where do you reckon we should go first eh?" Mary-Ann said, her chest bouncing with laughter.

"Well we aren't ready to go yet," Landon said with a sigh.

"We aren't?" she asked, turning her head to the side.

"Of course not. We need a crew of at least five others, and we won't be the only pirates on the water." Landon hopped down from the bed and began to pace back and forth as if walking the deck of a ship. "We need a cook. Someone that will make great food. What should their name be?" he asked, pointing the sword at Mary-Ann.

"Oh, you know I'm no good with names. If you didn't have that name tag on, I would keep forgetting yours." She let her hands fall on her lap, hopeless.

"No. Think really hard. What's a good name for a cook?"

Mary-Ann blew air through her nose like a pouting child. "Oh, I don't know. Uh...Carol. Why not Carol. That's a good name, don't you think?"

"A wonderful name. See, I knew you could do it." Landon paced back the other way, now walking with a limp, his peg leg tapping sharply on the floor. "Four more names. We need two men to man the sails and two men to load the cannons."

"Okay, let's see here. Luke and Prince. Those sound like the names of strong men who could man our sails." Mary-Ann suddenly sat higher in her chair, a sense of excitement exuding from her face. "And Paul and Aaron. They could shoot our cannons if another ship came our way."

"Perfect!" Landon shouted, standing up on the chair and pretending to look through a spyglass.

"One more thing before we set sail. All pirates have a nemesis. Another pirate who seeks the same treasure. Someone we must fight to find riches that will allow us to feed the hungry and give shelter to those in need." He jumped back down and stroked his chin in thought. "The evil pirate captain, Allan Slumpshoulder."

Mary-Ann burst, holding her hand in front of her mouth. "That sounds an awful lot like my husband," she said, reaching up to tickle him. "And let's say he's holding a pretty princess captive. Princess Stacey of—" Just like that, Mary-Ann's eyes drifted off to the other side of the room.

"Of Angel Land," Landon finished, springing back onto the bed.

Mary-Ann turned her attention back to the game, shaking her head as if she understood. I sat baffled, unable to believe what had happened myself. It had been months since Mary-Ann spoke the names of her children, and with the magic of this little boy, she brought them back without even knowing it.

"All aboard Mary-Ann's Delight," Landon exclaimed, standing up on the bed and pointing his sword. "We are heading east to Dark Beard Island in search of the greatest treasure this world has ever known."

Mary-Ann let out a hoot.

"Prince, Luke, man the sails. Carol, get below deck and start cooking us all something delicious. Paul, Aaron, load the cannons, we must be prepared to fight at any moment." Landon hopped back down and leaned in close to Mary-Ann. "Lieutenant, be my eyes on the horizon. Captain Slumpshoulder is bound to be out there." Waving his hand in an arching motion, Landon spun her wheelchair and began pushing her slowly around the room.

Mary-Ann held her hand up to her eye and peered through it, moving her head from side to side. "Nothing yet captain."

I felt a tap on my shoulder. Allan stood in the doorway with his hands on his hips. "Looks like they're having fun," he said, pulling the hallway chair into the room and having a seat.

"You wouldn't believe me if I told you," I said, handing him my notepad and crossing my arms. For a long while, Allan stared at the pages, flipping them back and forth in disbelief. "You're joking, right?" he asked, pointing at the names I'd circled. All I could do was shake my head.

"But how?" Allan handed the notepad back and I continued to write.

"It just happened. I don't know, but I can't make something like that up. It was like her family came rushing back all at once."

Landon wheeled her around in a circle and headed back towards the window. "I think I see a ship," Mary-Ann said, pointing out at the neighboring buildings.

"Let me check." Landon played at his spyglass again with a grunt. "Skull and crossbones on the banner. It must be Captain Slumpshoulder." *Captain Slumpshoulder, Captain Slumpshoulder,* the bird squawked.

Allan leaned over and asked, "Who is that?" a puzzled look drawn across his face. Snickering, I flipped back a few pages and pointed.

"Captain Allan Slumpshoulder," he read, letting out an airy laugh. "They just got the whole bunch of us didn't they." Shaking his head, he turned back to watch the show.

"Ready the cannons," Landon shouted turning their 'ship' sideways.

"Cannons ready captain," Mary-Ann exclaimed, lowering her voice to sound gruff.

Landon's breath quickened, and he darted back and forth quickly. "Steady. Wait for my signal." Mary-Ann twisted in her chair, sweat dripping from her brow in anticipation.

"Ready. Fire!" Landon ran back to the chair and gave it a nudge, acting as the backfire from the cannons. "Direct hit. We've done it lads. Ready yourself to board that pesky ship and save the princess." Paper sword in hand, Landon pretended to fight off an enemy, stabbing him through the heart. "Yield, Captain Slumpshoulder, or be sentenced to walk the plank," he said, pointing his sword at the wall.

Mary-Ann clear her throat and said, "Take my life if you will, but I will never yield."

"So be it. Captain Allan Slumpshoulder, I sentence you to die by the sea. Men, tie him up." Landon jumped over one of the chairs and knelt down. "Don't be afraid," he whispered, reaching out his hand. "Princess Stacey of Angel Land, you are safe with me. We will find our treasure and bring you back to your father, the king."

"Oh, thank you so much," Mary-Ann said, her voice soft and delicate. "I've never met a pirate that was so kind."

Landon stood and placed his hand over his heart. "We may be pirates, but we will never prey on the weak."

By this time, Nurse Benson, Nurse Proctor, Dr. Imish and Landon's mother Sherry, were all standing in the doorway. It was as if the room had transformed. We could smell the salt of the sea, hear the seagulls cawing overhead, and the sound of the waves crashing into the boat.

"I found this map, captain," Mary-Ann said, holding out her hands.

Landon took the map and examined it. "The location of the treasure is different from our map to this one," he said, holding it up to the light of the sun. "When we reach Dark Beard Island, we'll have to split up." Landon grabbed the wheelchair and pushed. "Full speed ahead boys," he shouted, pointing his sword. *Full speed ahead. Full speed ahead,* croaked Craggy.

The others leapt out of the way as Landon pushed Mary-Ann through the door and started down the hallway. Chasing close behind, we watched as they rounded the corner, nearly knocking over a nurse pushing a cart.

As they entered the main lobby, Landon slowed, pulling out his 'spyglass' and looking over at the chairs. "Land hooooo!" he shouted. *Land ho! Land ho!* "Drop the anchor." Mary-Ann threw her arms over the side of the chair, making a splashing sound as the anchor hit the water.

"Cook Carol. Guard the prisoner, see that he does not escape." Landon jumped onto the oval rug in the waiting room. "Lieutenant take Prince and Luke and follow this map. I will take the others and follow this one. Meet back here before the setting sun, and good luck." Landon took off to the left, crawling along the floor. He jumped to his feet, swinging his sword in a paranoid motion, his head jerking back and forth.

Dr. Imish was quick to move, stepping over and gently pushing Mary-Ann to the right. She searched the chairs, lifting cushions and setting aside pillows. As they made it to the wall, he turned and brought her back along the coffee tables in the middle of the room. She lifted a magazine, then another, her eyes growing wide and her mouth opening joyfully. Landon stomped along the floor, ignoring the two-people sitting in the room waiting to be seen. He rummaged under their chairs, then stood, giving them a stern look. The older of the two women returned his stare with even intensity, pulling her bag close and shooting her nose in the air with playful arrogance. Landon and Mary-Ann looked up at the sky. Seeing that the sun was floating behind the distant mountains, they made their way back to where the ship was anchored.

"I found nothing of value on my journey. His map must have been a fake," Landon complained, throwing his sword on the ground in disgust.

"Captain, his may have been a fake, but ours was not." Mary-Ann pretended to lift something with great weight. "I found this chest, but the lock is too strong for me to open."

Landon reached down and grabbed his sword. "Well done, Lieutenant." He raised the sword high above his head and slammed it back down against the lock. "No lock is too strong for me," he praised, sheathing the sword in the waistband of his shorts. Reaching forward, he lifted the lid. "You found it! Gold, silver and jewels," he said with excitement. Craggy squawked suddenly, *gold, silver and jewels. Gold, silver and jewels.* Jumping forward, Landon throwing his arms around Mary-Ann's neck.

They sailed back into the room, shouts of praise coming from everyone watching. "That was too much fun," Mary-Ann said, coming to a stop by the window.

Landon kissed her gently on the cheek and thanked her for being such a great lieutenant. He set his sword and his hat on the windowsill next to Mary-Ann's snow globe and left the room gripping the hand of his mother.

Chapter 16

May 5th, 2010

"Landon, you need to calm down," his mother said, holding onto his arms. Landon squirmed, tossing his head in all directions.

"But I want her to come. They said she could come." Tears streamed down his face, soaking the collar of his shirt.

"If she isn't feeling well, then she needs to stay here and rest."

"But it's my birthday and I want Mama to come with us. She said she would watch me play in the ball pit and hold onto my tickets. We were going to pick out a prize together." Landon fell into his mother's arm, his wailing echoing down the hallway.

"I know baby. But sometimes when people get really sick it's not safe for them to go outside."

"Then I want to stay here." He pushed her away and bolted around the corner.

Mary-Ann had developed a cough over the last several weeks and Nurse Proctor recommended she stay in bed, limiting the time she could spend with visitors. Allan agreed, sitting bedside most days and through the night. We heard fists pounding on the door and rushed down the hallway. As we turned the corner, Allan stood overtop a frightened Landon, his finger thrust into Landon's chest. "You need to leave. She's not feeling well and with all that noise you're going to wake her." Allan turned his head and saw that we were watching. Embarrassed, he went back inside.

Sherry fell to a knee as Landon walked back, sobbing into her arms. "It's alright sweetie. Mr. Cauldwell didn't mean that. He's just scared. Mary-Ann's not feeling well, and he's just scared."

I walked to the room and peered through the small window on the door. Mary-Ann was hooked to the respiratory, with an oxygen mask on her face and her body tightly wrapped in a blanket. Allan sat beside her, his head laying heavily on her arm. The dim light from a candle cast long shadows across the room.

My hand hesitated by the handle, my heart pounding anxiously. As I opened the door, Allan's head shot up. Though dark, I could see that he was crying.

"I'm only here for a second," I whispered, taking several steps forward.

"She's fading, Sal."

"What happened?" I asked as I rounded the bed and placed an arm on his shoulder.

"Her fever worsened a few days ago, and her body hasn't been able to fight it off. She started having trouble breathing so the doctors said it would be smart for her to rest." He turned back to Mary-Ann and reached up to caress her face.

"She'll pull through. I know it. Have you told your family?" I asked.

"I called Aaron earlier and he said he would let everyone know." He shook his head and collapsed back into Mary-ann's lap. "Now Landon is going to think I hate him."

"No, he'll be fine. Children get over things much easier than we do." I thought for a moment, flipping through pages in my head of all I had seen over the last two years. "How long has it been since Landon's seen her?" I asked.

"Other than the staff here at the hospital, I'm the only one that has been in here in over a week. I didn't want someone bringing in anything that might make things worse."

"I fully support that decision. I'm not saying the kid has special powers, but it is his birthday. Why don't you let him come in here and just talk to her?"

Allan picked up his head, dried tears glistening on his cheeks. "I guess that would be alright."

Out in the hallway, Landon sat with his back against the wall, a bowl of ice cream in his hands and smudges of vanilla on his nose, lips and chin. Sherry sat beside him, her knees pulled to her chest and her left-hand massaging Landon's neck.

"Mary-Ann wants to see you," I said as I knelt down beside him. His eyes grew wide and he set the bowl down on the ground. "Wait," I said, holding up my hand. "She is very ill, and she is still trying to rest but she said she wants you to tell her a story. Or talk about all the things you know because it will help her to feel better."

"I can do that. I can talk about a lot of things." Landon jumped to his feet and marched to Mary-Ann's room, pausing in the doorway. Walking behind him, I saw Allan standing by the bed looking down at his wife.

Allan looked up and motioned for Landon to enter. He walked around the bed and place a gentle hand on Landon's head. "I'm sorry, little guy. I didn't mean to scare you." He pulled him in and squeezed, planting a kiss on his forehead.

Allan and I sat by the door, a place we often found ourselves when at the hospital, watching what seemed like magic swirl around the room.

Gabriel Fowler

"Mary-Ann," Landon whispered as he approached the bed. "Mama. You go ahead and get some rest alright. Did you know that the average adult needs between seven and nine hours of sleep per night to perform well? I'm not sure why they don't just say eight hours, that is between the numbers seven and nine." Landon shrugged his shoulders, inching closer to the bed and resting his tiny hand on hers. Allan and I exchanged glances, the faintest smile touching his lips.

"But did you know that when you're asleep, your body is fighting some of the bad things inside you. So, when you're sick you need more rest." Landon slowly climbed onto the bed, sandwiching himself between Mary-Ann and the railing, laying his head on her shoulder. Allan tensed, fidgeting in his seat.

Leaning over, I whispered, "Let's just see what happens."

Landon wiggle next to her, then closed his eyes. "I'm ten today. You probably don't remember but I told you it was my birthday. We were supposed to go to Chuck E. Cheese and play games together. We were going to see if they had any snow globes there, so I could have one that matched yours. But you're not feeling well, and you know what, that's okay. I can wait and when you get better, we can go." Soon their breath rose and fell in unison.

"Salvador said I should tell you story." Landon turned on his side, draping his hand over her waist. "There once was a little girl who lived in a faraway land. She had long black hair that she tied into a braid and it hung over her shoulder like a snake. Her name was Abigail, but everyone else called her The Witch of the Wood.'"

"Her parents abandoned her as a little girl because she had one blue eye and one green eye. There was a prophecy telling of a child bearing this feature that would be the darkness of the world. She survived off the waters of the Yie River and plants and berries she found amongst the trees."

"It's hard to believe he's only ten years old," Allan whispered, his face stretched in disbelief.

"I know. This kid could be president one day," I said, making a note of the light flickering through the blinds.

"On her sixteenth birthday, Abigail ventured back into her village. You see, the prophecy said the darkness would come before she became a woman. When she returned, her village was empty, and smoke rose where there had once been straw homes." Landon yawned. "She found an old man dying by a tree who told her the king sent men..." he yawned again, his voice fading with each word. "The king..."

As his mouth closed, we could hear the gentle roll of air as it passed through his nose. "I supposed we can leave them be for now," Allan said as he struggled to his feet. "Captain Slumpshoulder could use a cup of coffee." He looked back at me and smiled.

"I hope you're not upset with me," Allan said to Sherry who was standing by the front desk. "I overreacted. I know he cares for her very much."

"Of course not. We share the same fears. Some days when Landon is connected to all the equipment, I worry it will be the last time I ever see him alive." Sherry gave Allan a hug. "Are they alright in there?" she asked.

"Yes, they're fine. He fell asleep telling her a story."

A thin line drew across her lips. "That sounds like Landon. The only time he's not talking is when he's asleep. As a matter-of-fact, that's not true. He's told a story or two in his sleep as well."

Allan nodded his head in understanding. "You've got a great kid. He's going to make a difference in this world, just like my Mary-Ann. It's so ironic that they found each other."

"I'll take healthy for now. We can talk about changing the world once we've dealt with that." A buzzer went off on Sherry's wrist. "I guess I can get a few hours of overtime since we won't be taking Landon out tonight. That is if you're okay with leaving him in there?"

"Yes, of course. He'll be fine. Sal and I are going to grab a cup of coffee."

"Alright. I'll be back up in a few hours. Thanks again, he really needed this."

"As did she," Allan said, waving as Sherry left.

◇

"You won't believe this," Allan said the following afternoon.

I sat in my office making edits on a transit piece I had been working on and shut my computer. "What's going on?"

"I came in this morning to check on Mary-Ann and she was sitting in the hallway with Landon playing go fish. I heard her laugh from down the hallway. This kid's an angel sent from heaven."

"I'm starting to believe that myself," I said, scribbling a few notes.

"Join us tonight at five for Landon's birthday dinner."

"Chuck E. Cheese," I said sarcastically. "Can't say I've ever stepped foot in that place, but when Landon and Mary-Ann are together, amazing things happen. I'll see you there."

By the time four-thirty rolled around, I was knee deep in edits and needed a break. Collecting my things, I raced down the stairs and caught the train north. A giant mouse greeted me at the door with a smile, and a hug, which was rather unwanted on my part. But, I smiled, feeling sorry for the person stuck inside and walked to the table.

Landon sat at the edge of the booth, with Mary-Ann on the end in her wheelchair. His cheeks were covered in red sauce as he stuffed pizza into his mouth. Allan helped Mary-Ann eat, patiently holding the fork in front of her lips.

"Hello Salvador," Landon said with his mouth full.

I waved, then removed my jacket and sat in the booth next to them across from Aaron, who I was surprised to see was there.

"Allan didn't say you were coming," I said, reaching out to shake his hand.

"I wasn't planning on it, but my wife decided she wanted to go to a show tonight with some of her girlfriends." He wiped his face with a napkin. "Rather than sit at home alone—" he said with a shrug.

"I'm glad you did. Landon and your mother have really gotten on well." I took a plate from the table and served myself.

"Yeah, my father told me. 'Angel from heaven,' he keeps saying." Aaron shook his head in disbelief.

"Don't doubt it quite yet," I said with a smile, taking a bite of my pizza.

"Are you ready?" Landon said, sliding from his seat. His mother was quick to wipe his hands and face and it was a clear reminder that he was still, only ten years old.

Mary-Ann turned to Allan, her eyes like that of a child asking their parent if they could be excused from the table. Her brittle hands quivered as she took one of Allan's in hers. "Thank you," she whispered.

Allan leaned forward and planted a kiss on her cheek, then turned to Landon and smiled. "She's all yours little man."

Landon pulled the sleeves of his three quarter, black and white t-shirt up to his elbows, and adjust his hat before heading toward the ball pit. He weaved Mary-Ann in and out of games, their lights flashing and voices calling out for them to play. Landon struggle for a moment to lock her wheels, then, taking a few steps back, he sprinted forward, landing belly first into the rainbow. We could hear Mary-Ann's laugh amidst the games, her head rolling back and forth with joy. Aaron's expression shifted away from doubt, the corners of his lips twitching, making small divots in his cheeks.

Landon burst up through the balls, his mouth wide, screeching like a ferocious animal. "I wish you could jump in with me," he said, trudging back over to the edge. "Did you know that these used to be called a, *ball crawl*. A guy name Eric McMillan invented them in the 1970s. He said that the traditional playground was more like a graveyard and that adults had forgotten how to have fun." He tossed a ball into Mary-Ann's lap.

"What is this?" she asked, holding it in her hand.

"Duh, it's a ball," he said as he climbed out. "You hold onto that, it will be good luck when we play the games."

We all watch for the next hour as the two went from game to game. Landon danced in circles around her chair, stashing the tickets he'd win on her lap next to their lucky ball. Mary-Ann would cheer him on, chant his name and move her body as she'd watch balls drop, and machines push, hoping to win the jackpot. Out of coins and panting, Landon pushed her back to the table holding a piece of paper.

"What do you have there?" Sherry asked. Landon handed her the paper and sat, taking a huge gulp of soda. "Fourteen thousand two-hundred and six tickets," she said, her eyes growing wide.

"Yup. I told you it was a lucky ball, Mama. Now we need to go see what prizes they have." Landon snatched the ticket out of his mother's hand, hoped to his feet and pushed Mary-Ann to the back corner of the building.

Large stuffed animals hung from the wall next to remote controlled cars, lava lamps next to sling shots and bouncy balls next to tiny pieces of candy. A tall man with light brown hair stood behind the counter holding a stick with a hook at the end.

"Do you have your slip?" he asked, holding out his hand.

Landon gave it to him and leaned on the glass, looking at all the prizes. "Do you have any snow globes?" Landon asked.

"That's not much of a toy. We have an RC car, a balloon hammer." He walked to the end of the counter. "We also have this cool transformer. It goes from car, to robot, to boxing glove."

Landon stared at him with a blank expression. "But do you have any snow globes?"

Confused, the man slid one of the doors of the counter and pulled out a snow globe half the size of Mary-Ann's. "Eight thousand. It's not really worth the tickets buddy. You're better off going with--"

"I'll take it. And four of those candies and the sticky hand thing," he said, pointed through the glass.

With a shrug, the man dropped the prizes into the bag and handed it to Landon. "Look!" Landon shouted as he returned. "It's just like Mary-Ann's, only smaller." He shook the snow globe and watched with wonder as the flakes fell around the city scape.

Aaron nudged me on the arm and said, "I wish the rest of my family were here to see this. We haven't seen her smile like that in almost a year. The kid really is something special."

Smiling, I turned back as Landon fell softly into Mary-Ann's lap, giggling as she poked at his sides. "You're going to make me pee," Landon shouted. He rolled onto the floor trying to catch his breath. As he stood, he narrowed his brow and stuck his tongue out at Mary-Ann.

"You'd better watch it or that thing is going to be mine," she snickered, opening and closing her hand like a claw. Landon giggled. He walked to the table and upended the contents of the bag.

"Look what we got," he said, spreading them around. "Do you want a piece of candy? I got one for each of us."

Mary-Ann shook her head and said, "No sweetheart, you can have them both." Excited, Landon stuffed one into his mouth and the other into his pocket.

"It's starting to get late," Sherry said, pushing all the plates to the center of the table. "I'm going to go ask for a box for the leftover pizza."

"What about the cake?" Landon asked as she stepped out of the booth.

"Cake and presents back at the hospital remember," Michael said. It was odd because it was the first time I had heard him speak. His voice was soft and airy, the ends of his words drifting to nothing.

"Oh yeah, now I remember." Landon shook the snow globe and set it back down on the table. I watched as Mary-Ann's eyes floated away from the flashing lights and landed on the falling flecks of snow. It was as if her world had fallen still and sound longer existed. It was just her and a sense of weightlessness. I wondered then what it felt like, to be absent amidst a chaotic world.

"This was nice." Aaron said.

"I'm sure your brothers and sisters will be happy to hear how the night went," I said.

"Absolutely. I've sent a few pictures throughout the evening already." Aaron stood and shook my hand before saying happy birthday and hugging Mary-Ann and Allan. Landon waved happily, his toy sticky hand, stuck to his cheek as Aaron walked away.

"Alright everyone, we'll meet you back at the hospital for dessert and gifts," Sherry said as she closed the pizza box.

After helping Mary-Ann into Allan's car, I pulled him to the side. "I'd love to head back with you, but unfortunately work is piling up on my desk as we speak. Give this to Landon for me, would

Gabriel Fowler

you?" I said, handing him a small gift bag. "It's not much, but I hope he likes it."

As I walked back to the train station, I wondered what his reaction would be as he read the title of the book I had gotten him. <u>A Thousand Things to Know for No Reason.</u> The book of facts *he* was, I imagined he would like it very much.

Chapter 17

August 4, 2010

Landon lay in his hospital bed with his head wrapped in a moist towel. His skin gripped the edges of his bones, almost translucent against its hard surface. We could see the thin blue veins as they dove across his eyelids. The last round of chemotherapy left him weak and brittle, struggling to move and eat, the weight of the sickness crushing him into a coma-like sleep.

Michael draped his arms over Sherry's shoulders as they sat bedside, her tears soaking into Landon's lap. Mary-Ann and Allan sat opposite them. Allan squeezed his eyes shut, his lips twitching in prayer as Mary-Ann held Landon's hand, her soft whispers floating like feathers above him. Although sunlight poured through the windows, the room felt dark and cold, a cloud of sadness hanging over.

"Come back to us, please." Sherry clung harder to Landon's arm to will his strength back.

As I sat in the chair along the back wall, only the sound of Landon's heart monitor sang, the intensity of its beat like the faint thump of distant footsteps. For over an hour we sat, the shadows in the room changing as each cloud rolled passed the sun.

"Allan." My pad and pen slid to the floor as I stood, my steps like walking on cracking ice. "Allan," I said a little louder, a franticness creeping into my throat. My hand rose slowly, index finger shaking as it found its place on Mary-Ann. The left side of her face began to slump, as if the skin was being pulled from her cheek. Her head fell like a weight, her body cascading forward into Landon's bed.

"What's happening?" Allan shouted, reaching forward to pull her back up.

"Nurse!" Michael rushed to the door and waved down Nurse Benson. "Something's wrong." He pushed his way into the room and knelt at Mary-Ann's side.

"We need to get her out of here, now." He ran to the adjacent room and returned with a bed. "Help me get her on here."

I'm unsure of its madness, or its miracle. The weightless body of a woman who'd lived a full life being pushed on a gurney, the frantic cry of her husband as he slowly trailed behind. The sound of a young boy's heart monitor gained strength, a war drum thundering as if an army were approaching. Was it in some way a trade? Or, was it her final gift, the last of her strength rolling from her like beads of sweat into his fragile bones?

Thinking quickly, I took Mary-Ann's wheelchair and caught Allan before he reached the door. "Sit, we'll get there faster." People moved aside as we marched down the hallway. A silence fell over us, similar to the way the city sounds when you listen to everything all at once. The bodies of nurses, doctors and patients became a blur.

When we reached the emergency room, Mary-Ann lay still on the bed, her shirt cut down the middle and pads placed around her chest. Allan reached forward, helplessness dripping from each finger, his eyes an empty well, having shed his last for Landon.

"Is she...please. Not like this," he said, his words tearing within his throat. Nurse Benson stepped away from the bed.

"Nurse," I said, trying to hold Allan in the chair. I leaned down and said, "Let's get you into the hallway."

"No, I should be in there. She needs me." Allan pushed my arm away, grinding his teeth viciously.

"Mary-Ann is in the best hands right now. Let's go into the hallway and I can try and explain what happened." Nurse Benson was finally able to calm him, guiding Allan back into the wheelchair and into the hallway.

"Is she dead?" Allan asked, tearing at his shirt.

"No. Thankfully she was already here at the hospital. She suffered a massive stroke, and in her condition, we also believe it triggered a major heart attack." He ran his hand through his hair, exhaling deeply. "Your wife is the strongest woman I've ever met. They were able to stabilize her for now, but she'll need emergency surgery if she's going to survive much longer."

Somewhere deep in the belly of his soul, Allan found a pocket of tears. "Do whatever it takes," he said, a mountain of sorrow rushing from his eyes. He fell back in the chair, the pain making it impossible for him to move.

"I'll stay with him. You should call the family." Nurse Benson's attempt at comfort within those words was valiant, his eyes gentle, his forehead wrinkle with compassion and his chin pushing up toward his lips.

As I walked back down the hallway, the world around me came crashing in. The sounds of shouting, the clang of hospital carts, and the smell of sickness was overwhelming. Disoriented, I stumbled my way outside. For the first time, with hands clenched and throat dry, I broke. No, I shattered. I could feel every part of my body falling away as I fell heavily into the brick pillar. Unbeknownst to me, but eight years of grief was tearing me in every direction. I had never truly said goodbye to my father. I had been trying to hold onto something that was no longer there. As I sobbed, with the timid faces of onlookers walking by, I was reminded of that line in the poem Allan had shown me. *The best of me is gone.* And I was reminded of my pursuit to prove it wrong. With my body shaking, and tears rushing down my face, I took a deep breath, allowing the relief to wash over me as I finally said goodbye to my father. Standing, I pulled my phone from my pocket, wiped my nose with the sleeve of my shirt, and called Prince.

"What do you mean?" I could hear the terror in his voice.

"It's what I was told. I'll call Aaron, but you should get here as quick as you can."

My feet slid across the floor as I made it back to where Allan was sitting. "Aaron is on his way," I said, falling into the seat next to him. "How is she?"

Nurse Benson shook his head, his eyes drifting toward the ground. "She's still in surgery."

"Landon," Allan said suddenly. "She would want someone to go check on him." I volunteered, leaving my phone with Allan in case Aaron tried to call. Landon's room had a glow of promise as I walked through the door. His parents stood together, their arms in a tangle listening to the doctor.

"Compared to his condition this morning, he seems to be doing much better." The doctor wrote something on his clipboard. "We'll continue to monitor his progress, but this is a very good sign." Nodding, he turned and left the room.

Landon's color was slowly coming back, his bones lessening their tension. Sherry looked at me with eyes that were filling with life, her smile faint, but present. "He's coming back," she said. Exhaling, she sat, her head falling back on Landon's lap.

"What happened to Mary-Ann?" Michael asked.

"She suffered another stroke and they believe this one may have triggered a heart attack. She was rushed into surgery."

"Oh, no." Sherry stood again, wrapping her arms around Michael's neck. "When can we see her?" he asked.

I shrugged my shoulders. "I can't imagine it would be any time soon, but Allan asked if I would check in on Landon. It's what Mary-Ann would have wanted." I walked slowly to the bed and laid my hand gently on his forehead. His skin was still warm from the fever, but his breath was strong.

"Allan will be pleased to hear he's doing well," I said.

"Tell him that we will be by to see Mary-
Ann the second she comes out of surgery," Sherry
said, wiping her face with her hands.

"I will."

I paused in the doorway to listen to the
sound of his heartbeat, the raging army charging
into battle. A fight to stay alive, to be victorious, to
change the world.

I met Aaron in the hallway as I made my
way back to the emergency room, with Andrea
following close behind.

"How did it happen?" he asked, tugging on
my arm.

"We were in Landon's room. Your mother
was praying over him when suddenly, she
collapsed." We took a left down another hallway,
passing by a pregnant woman, and a teen holding an
icepack to his head. After another left, we pushed
through a set of double doors and found Allan
speaking with a doctor. The doctor held his mesh
hat in his hand, and it looked as though he was
shaking his head, his face pinched solemnly.

"What do you mean she might not wake
up?" Allan asked, grasping the doctor's coat. His
strength was gone, and his words disappeared as
they reached his lips, like an echo falling down a
well.

"Sit, Dad. Please," Aaron said. He stood at his side and gingerly placed him back in the wheelchair.

"We were able to repair the collapsed valve in her heart, but unfortunately, she may not be strong enough to survive the recovery." The doctor let his arms fall to his sides. "I'm terribly sorry."

"Can we go see her?" Aaron asked.

"Yes, of course. Follow me." He led us through a pair of swinging doors and into the recovery room. Blue curtains hung from the ceiling separating patients from each other. Nurses huddled near a small computer drinking coffee and looking over charts.

Allan reached for her hand, kissing it gently, and cupping his face within her palm. Andrea nestled her head into Aaron chest, her arms wrapping around his waist. As odd as it may seem, and the simple fact that I had just said goodbye to my father; I felt him there, an arm draped over my shoulder like when I was young boy admiring a science project we had worked on together. And as I looked down at Mary-Ann connected to all the equipment, I knew, that if this was the end, I could help them say goodbye as well.

◇

Remember Me

Mary-Ann's heart continued to beat hours into the night, and they moved her to her own room. I offered to ride with Aaron to the airport to pick up Prince and his family, while Andrea stayed behind with Allan. The night air was cool, and a soft breeze floated through the folds of my shirt. The sky sparkled white on a black canvas, displaying the universe in its glory. As we climbed into his car, I noticed his dashboard was covered in small, white slips of paper. My eyes went from them, to him, and back to the papers.

"You were right," he said as he turned the key.

"Right about what?"

"This wasn't about her leaving. It was remembering that she was still there all along. And these papers remind me of that each and every day."

I leaned forward and read the nearest one. *My son fell off his bike and you were there to blow on his knee and tell him everything was going to be alright. It also helped that you had a superman bandage. Thank you, Mama.*

Inspired, I reached into my pocket for a pen. Tearing off a page of my wallet note pad, I wrote one of my own. *Because of you, I was able to finally say goodbye to my father. Because of you, I look at the world through a different lens, admiring the talents of those around me, and sharing the talents I have with those in need. Thank you, Mama. I love you.*

I handed it to Aaron and he read, nodding his head.

The rolling tires were the only sound that invaded the air inside the car until we parked at the airport. Aaron unbuckled his seatbelt and let out a weighted sigh, letting his head crash heavily into the headrest. "This is the hardest thing I've ever had to do."

After a long pause, I said, "But we are all doing it together."

Prince and his family were waiting outside the terminal as we were walking up. "I tried calling both of you," Prince said.

Aaron and I felt our pockets, gasping at the realization. "I left mine with your father hours ago in case anyone called."

"And mine is in Andrea's purse. Sorry." Aaron stepped in and wrapped his arms around his brother.

"Is she…"

"No, she's still alive." Aaron stepped back, his hands still gripping Prince's shoulders. "The doctor said she's stable, but she may never wake."

"Can she still hear us?" Prince asked, a touch of pain tugging at his words.

Aaron's arms fell to his sides. "There's no genuine answer to that, but we are going to talk to her either way."

"Yeah, of course."

After greeting each of them, I took Elizabeth's bags and they followed us to the car. "You said something about the kid on the phone, Sal?" Prince said as we reached the highway.

"Yeah. He had gotten really sick after his treatment. We were all in Landon's room supporting his parents. I sat off to the side, taking notes for the book when Mary-Ann collapsed. No one realized it until I said something and within minutes, she was being rushed to the emergency room."

"And the boy?" Prince said, turning around in the front seat. "Is he alright?"

"The last I checked he was gaining strength and starting to recover." I shook my head, looking out the window at the stars. "I've said this before, but I swear those two have some sort of connection. Like they were meant to find each other."

"How do you mean?" Isaiah said.

"The more time they spent together, the better Mary-Ann got. But when Landon got sick, it was as if she sacrificed herself to save him. I know it sounds crazy, but…"

The car fell silent, as if contemplating the idea that it might be true. She was that kind of person after all. When we arrived back at Mary-Ann's room, Sherry and Michael were standing outside with Andrea.

"Is everything alright?" Aaron asked as we approached.

"Yes," Andrea said. "Nothing has changed. We just thought it would be a good idea to give your father some time alone with her."

Prince peeked through the window. "I'm going to go in and see her." The door opened with a faint squeak.

I watched through the window. Prince bent and embraced his father, then walked to the other side of the bed and sat. After a short while, we could hear the muffled sound of *Amazing Grace*. Prince swayed back and forth, his mother's hand in his.

"You should be in there too," I said, nudging Aaron forward. As he walked in, I took a seat on the floor of the hallway, my knees tucked into my chest, the weight of a thousand days rolled all into one.

Two days later, Michael rolled Landon in his wheelchair through the double doors and into Mary-Ann's room. Paul, Carol, Stacey, Luke, Aaron and Prince were there as well, holding hands and singing. Allan rested his cheek on Mary-Ann's shoulder, gently humming into her ear. Flowers brought by community members covered the floor, and from the ceiling, hung hundreds of letters.

Michael pushed Landon beside her bed. In his lap was her snow globe, the specks of white floating weightlessly beneath the glass. With tears in his eyes, Landon set the snow globe by her feet, then sat back and listened quietly as they sang.

I stood in the doorway and felt a light tug on my shirt. Turning, I found Katrina standing with a small vase of white roses. "Thank you for calling," she whispered, planting a kiss on my neck.

Nodding, I hung my arm around her shoulder, pulling her in close to feel her warmth.

As the song faded, Allan lifted his head, his eyes glistening with tears. "Thank you all for being here. Our family is the most important thing in this world." He waved Landon over and lifted him onto his lap. "Is there anything you would like to say to her?"

Landon thought for a moment, rubbing the back of his scalp. "I'm glad I met you. And, I hope you'll find a real treasure one day. I love you Mama." He fell back into Allan's arms, wrapped himself around Allan's neck and whimpered.

One day he would realize that her real treasure were the people standing in that room.

On the fourth day, we listened as the ring of Mary-Ann's heartbeat eventually faded to nothing. She never woke, her hands folded over her waist, her body calm, like she was floating on the water's surface. But just as she entered this earth, she left it, with her lips tightened in a thin line.

A smile that would carry on for generations to come.

CPSIA information can be obtained
at www.ICGtesting.com
Printed in the USA
LVHW111719120919
630868LV00006B/846/P

9 781949 472639